ISBN-13: 9798402504127
ISBN-10: 1477123456

Cover design by: Sonya Sutherland
Library of Congress Control Number: 2018675309
Printed in the United States of America

OUTSIDE THE PICKET FENCE

by

Sonya Sutherland

1

I blink a stained white ceiling into focus. Hauling myself upright I look around, nothing is familiar. As I scoot to the edge of the bed, my hands, shoulders and hips are stiff and uncoordinated.

The room is sparsely decorated, a few pictures hang on the walls but I can't make them out in the dim light. A worn recliner and small table are clustered together in front of a flat T.V. My eyes settle at the window where a red glow leaks through the edge of dark heavy curtains.

Where am I?

I think back to try to connect the dots between what I see and where I am. In the distance there's a faint beeping, then hurried footsteps and the door flies open.

"Doris," an exasperated woman breathes as she flicks on the light, "you're up early."

I recoil and shield my eyes at the drastic change in light and her abrupt arrival.

Words gather slowly in my head but before I can speak she yells back through the doorway. "Can someone get the alarm!" Turning towards me, her large bosom heaves as she tries to catch her breath.

Who is this woman?

Her dark hair is pulled into a tight bun. Her ruddy, slightly sagging skin suggests she isn't young. She seems familiar but something about her makes me uneasy. There are no formalities or greetings. I watch the woman, my mind spins as I try to place her. The silver pin on her shirt reads KAY.

Kay makes her way to a tall dresser and starts to pull out pieces of clothing. Large black letters label the top drawer, "DORIS' UNDERWEAR." My name is repeated on the drawers below.

The dresser contains my things. Why is she in my things?

"Get out of there!" I stand quickly, almost losing my balance. She rushes towards me and grabs my arm.

"Doris calm down, no one wants a fall. We just need to get you dressed."

My eyes fall to the faded yellow nightgown I'm wearing. I shake her off of me and head toward the dresser. The beeping sound from the hallway continues.

"Gavin, I got her, can you get the alarm!" The beeping stops. "Thank goodness," she mutters to herself.

Alarm?

Am I being held here?

I take a deep breath. My mind is sluggish as I try to focus. Distracted, I rub my toes into the worn carpet and I become aware of pressure in my bladder.

There is urgency and my eyes dart around the room. I don't see what I'm looking for so I take a few steps toward the open doorway.

"Oh no, Doris, you need to stay here and get dressed." She

reaches for my arm again and starts to pull me back toward the bed. "We aren't ready down at breakfast for you yet."

In the distance another beeping sound begins. The woman mutters, "I guess everyone's up early this morning."

My brain swirls as I try to collect my thoughts. It takes great effort but I finally spit out a word, "bathroom."

The woman groans. She releases my arm and walks to the far corner of the room. She drags a large white seat from behind a screen decorated with Asian lilies.

"Fine, this will be quicker, hurry up." She points to the seat.

I can't imagine what she means. I try to back toward the door but she pulls me forward holding my hand tightly.

The pressure builds, I start to sweat. I know where I want to go and this isn't it. My words and thoughts won't come together.

She impatiently lifts the white lid, revealing the commode for what it is. Still I stare. I can't understand the lack of privacy. Maybe it's all part of the punishment, my incarceration. I step forward and she pulls down my bottoms.

I sit. I let go. There is relief, warmth and shame.

#

Seated at a long wooden table, I take a deep breath and debate my next move. I've been given a small cup of pills and a tall glass of water.

There are three pills, two tiny round ones in shades of pink and one large white oblong one. They don't look menacing, almost cheerful, but I know they're what keep the thoughts from coming together. It's how they keep me complacent.

I look around the dining room. It's small with a half wall connecting it to the kitchen so we are never out of sight. Attempts to create a "cozy" feel are scattered about the ranch home. Above the sink hangs an orange and brown painting of a field of sunflowers, while a set of three wood butterfly carvings dance along a paneled wall. The white candle flickering on the counter says vanilla on the jar but all I can smell is coffee and bleach.

Across from me sits a dark haired woman, her thick tresses are pulled up in a tight bun. A silver pin that reads "KAY" flashes on her chest as she chuckles at the comic section of the newspaper. To my left, is an old man in a black sweatsuit pretending to sleep. I can tell he's pretending because he occasionally lifts his wooly eyebrows and looks cautiously around the room. When our eyes meet, he winks.

He is the same as me. The man in black and I both pretend to conform, to get through the day in this place.

"Doris," the dark haired woman startles me with her gregarious voice. "Take your meds. You'll have a visitor today after breakfast!" She adds a smile to the end of her statement and raises her pencil thin eyebrows in feigned excitement.

I can't decide if it's a statement or an ultimatum, so I put the pills in my mouth and drink the water. My tongue feels fat and doesn't want to allow the pills to pass. I cough a little and water dribbles down my chin.

"Come on Doris, don't be difficult," the woman groans getting up from her chair. She approaches me with her silver name tag shining brightly.

She leans down and gently holds my chin, tipping my head back. I take a breath just before she pours more water into my partially open mouth. I swallow hard, clutching the hand holding my chin.

She lets go and I take a gasping breath.

"There now, let me see."

I open my mouth and say "ahhh," out of habit.

"Good girl," she pats my cheek.

I glare at her as she returns to her seat and flips the newspaper back up between us.

#

"Why don't you find a seat hon." Kay waves her hand in the general direction of a recliner and a couch.

I half plop onto the couch. It's low and takes such great effort to settle into that I'm not sure I'll be able to get back up. Everything is brown in here. It feels dark and I wish I had thought to open a curtain before I sat. Huge faces fill the large television screen but the volume is so low it's hard to hear what they're saying.

"Doris, look who's here!" Kay booms from the hallway. She's followed by a man who is slightly younger than her carrying a brown paper bag. He has a hesitant look on his face, his dark eyebrows raised in expectation and his mouth pursed in a slightly nervous smile.

I should know him. I feel close to him and I want to reach out to him. His presence makes me feel both sad and comforted. I wish I knew him.

He puts the bag on the floor before he sits next to me on the couch and touches my hand, his mouth breaks into a true smile, "Hi, Mom."

Finally I find him in my mind, his smile shines a light in my memory and I'm triumphant.

"Scott!" I declare proudly.

He laughs a little. "How are you, Mom?"

I wonder if I should be honest, if the truth will help or make things worse. I don't want to worry him.

"Well, I'm here, can't complain I guess."

He reaches into the bag and pulls out a fuzzy green bundle with a pair of bright pink slippers on top. "I brought a new robe for you and some slippers, I heard you can't find yours."

"It's not that I can't find them, it's that they keep taking them!" I'm speaking too loudly, Kay looks up from her reading and frowns.

I hush my voice and lean in towards Scott. I glance suspiciously at Kay and before I can stop myself, the words come rushing out.

"It's that these people want to punish me. I know it's their job and I try not to let them get to me but..." My lip is trembling. "I'm sorry."

I grab both of Scott's hands in mine. "Please, I'll try to be better. I want to go home." Tears are falling now and I can't stop them.

Scott looks away, his voice sounds hollow. "I know Mom, I'm sorry. No one wants to punish you. You live here, this is your home."

I let go of his hands. Why would I live here? I pull a handkerchief from my sleeve and wipe my face.

Scott clears his throat and gives me a tight smile. "Anyway, how about we try these on and make sure they fit?"

He puts the slippers on the floor and shakes out the robe before he stands. The flash of fuzz and color take me by surprise and I smile. Scooting to the edge of the deep couch, I try to push to stand but only manage to bounce. Scott laughs and takes me by the hand, gently lifting me up.

He wraps the robe around me and plants a quick peck on my cheek. Giggling, I pull it tight enjoying its softness. I slide my stocking feet under the single wide strap of each pink slipper and take a few steps.

"Looking good Mom!"

"Thank you." I smile.

Scott leans in and gives me a long hug, "I just want you to be happy Mom."

I close my eyes and breathe in the smell of soap and fabric softener. "Oh, I am." I say feeling warm and safe.

#

(April 1957)

My palm is damp with sweat while Paul and I hold hands strolling down the sidewalk on our way home from school. He walks with me every day even though he lives a few blocks in the other direction. Paul is a year older than me, close to graduating. Some girls think he looks like Paul Newman. When I told him this, he blushed and rolled his eyes. I like that he isn't full of himself. Not because he isn't confident but because he doesn't have to brag for people to see what is good about him.

I squeeze his hand. He looks at me and smiles. The sun is warm and a gentle breeze brings the faint smell of lilac. I find myself walking slower as we get closer to my block. I love spending time with him being a regular teenager. The moments with Paul between the end of school and when we arrive at my gate are a welcome break between two harsh realities. It seems to be the only place I fit in.

"Doris, do you think you could come out to the Chick Inn

for a burger later?" He looks hopeful.

"I can't, chores." I lie, disappointing myself.

I want to explain more but I don't, because although Paul knows my family is poor, I'm not sure he needs to know we are broken as well.

I envy Paul. I want what he has, a nice respected family with a cute house and a white picket fence. I hope that by being close to him, a little bit of that normal life will rub off on me.

What I really hope is that Paul will give me his ring and, after we both graduate, we can get out of here together. I'm not sure what to expect though. Paul hasn't ever talked about leaving Ypsilanti, or about any of his plans after graduation. But I hold onto the dream of leaving this town and he is the best thing I have going for me.

When we turn onto my block the street is unusually empty and quiet. No one is sitting on their porch smoking. There are no children out riding bikes or playing.

A loud metal bang cuts the silence of the street. The screen door of my small grey house swings in the breeze, carelessly slapping against the black iron railing. I drop Paul's hand.

"OK, thanks. I better get in." I walk quickly toward the iron gate.

Bang! The door claps again.

"Wait, Doris, I wanted to...."

Bang! The breeze catches the door and cuts him off.

"No, I really need to get inside Paul." I pull firmly on the stiff gate.

"But Doris..." He holds out my books.

Bang!

I reach to take the books, and again a gust of wind slams

the door loudly against the rail. I catch my breath.

Paul starts to speak again but stops with his mouth frozen, still forming a word. Looking past me, he stares at the house.

I turn to see my father, shirtless, in the doorway. He stumbles a little, trying to grab the door then falls forward.

His large hand pushes through the screen. He cannot stop the momentum. His whole body flails as his weight rips the door from its hinges.

"Ahhhhgh," he slurs loudly as he falls with a mix of pain and surprise.

He and the door are now in a tangled heap on the stoop. His face is pathetic and innocent as he stares toward me at the gate.

Paul looks from my father to me and back.

"Dorish, Dorish, oh God, help me!" My father yells from under the pile of aluminum. He is so loud, I know this is why the neighbors have called their children in.

"OK, Paul, Bye." I start to close the gate but when I try to pull I almost shut Paul in it. I look at him in surprise.

"He's big, I'll help," he quietly steps into the yard.

I don't know how to refuse. My insides burn with embarrassment. I can't say anything, but manage a nod.

We walk up the steps, I grab my father under one shoulder while Paul grabs the other arm. I can't look at him. Paul counts to three and we yank up. My father manages to get his feet under him and as he rises he notices Paul for the first time.

"Hey!" He yells, with his face swaying inches from Paul's.

"You're Gregg's boy!" He grabs Paul's shoulder and gives it a shake. "Goodboy, youtellyur ole man I say hi, Gregg, Gregg..."

He mutters and turns around.

He gets his feet tangled in the screen again and almost falls back into the house. He clings to the door jamb. "C'mon Dorish, yermothers gone, I think it's time to eat."

"Thanks, Paul," I step over the crumpled screen into the house.

Paul grabs my hand and speaks softly. "I'll see you tomorrow."

I don't look up until Paul is at the gate, I manage a small wave that I don't think he sees. I push the heavy wood door shut and lean my back against it.

"Dorish!" My father calls from the living room. I cringe and take a deep breath.

My brother sometimes teases that my father's pet name for me is "Dorish" since that's what he calls me when he's drunk. We joke that he has his own language because an entire sentence can come out slurred into one word, which is unintelligible to those who don't speak what we call "drunkish."

"Wheresumother?" he whimpers from the couch where he rubs the nubs that used to be fingers on his right hand.

He served in the last year of WWII, returned with a few missing fingers, a love for whiskey and an inability to keep a job.

"I don't know, Dad. I just got home," I say trying not to be short or let my anger show. I see a few scrapes on his forearm that are starting to bleed.

I grab a towel from the kitchen and toss it at him. He picks it up from the floor, pats gingerly at his arm, and whimpers again. I roll my eyes and return to the kitchen to pick through the cupboards. Before I get far, my mother bustles through the back door.

"There's soup in the freezer if that is what you're looking

for. It's not even dinner time though," She looks anxiously toward the TV room, "but I suppose he's hungry."

She flops her purse on the table, her eyes meet mine. I feel the slight sting of tears, I consider telling her what happened.

That the useless baby she chose as a husband had come crashing from the house to flaunt his drunkenness. Not only to the neighborhood, but to Paul.

How can I face him tomorrow? What should I do, Mom? I almost ask, my lip trembles.

She steps towards me and I start to open my arms ready for her embrace, but she only reaches to pull a towel from the oven handle.

"Why don't you take care of the mess on the front porch. I'll finish up with your father." She brushes by me on her way to him.

I take a deep breath and swallow hard at the lump in my throat. I blink furiously to clear my vision and squeeze my hands into tight fists.

I stomp to the front porch and kick the detached screen door which sends it sliding noisily down the steps.

A couple houses down, three girls play jump rope on the sidewalk. They don't look my way, their giggles drown the racket from the door. I drag the mangled aluminum carcass around the corner of the house, behind the fence and out of sight.

#

(June 1957)

From the roof of Paul's back porch, I look up at the stars. I'm just outside his bedroom window on the soft green blanket his mom knit for him.

Paul is inside going through his nighttime routine. Soon he'll come into his room, his face scrubbed and teeth brushed. He'll probably be wearing a white t-shirt and pajama pants his mother made him. She'll follow him in and kiss his forehead before he gets into bed. When she leaves, she'll turn out the light and the stars will become brighter for a moment.

I will wait, and he will wait, until the house is quiet. I don't mind waiting. Being so close to something so normal is comforting in itself. When his parents are tucked away in the front room watching television, he'll come to the window and climb out. We'll whisper to each other, hold each other, kiss, touch and wonder.

On this night, Paul is red faced when he enters his room, he looks agitated and rolls his eyes before he comes to the window and shuts the curtains.

This has never happened before, I'm not sure what I'm supposed to do. Should I leave? Does he want me to go?

Before I make any decisions I hear Paul's mother speaking loudly "I'm sorry Paul, your father and I have decided. This is what's going to happen, you'll get on fine. You'll just have to give it a chance."

I hear a loud groan from Paul, and then I hear the door slam shut. His light goes out and there's a different type of quiet, the kind that comes from confrontation.

I can't decide what I should do. I feel like I'm eavesdropping. I'm worried that Paul will be mad that I was a witness to this leak of emotion.

This small outburst seems larger than the noise and disruption that is typical at my house. It's not something that belongs here.

I begin to fold up the blanket to leave outside his window when Paul opens his curtains and peers outside. I'm not sure if he can see me so I give a little wave and he waves back.

He slides the window up slowly and slips outside.

"Where are you going?" He whispers with concern as he shuts the window halfway.

"I wasn't sure if I was meant to stay or if I should go."

Paul breathes deep and scoots closer to me, "Stay. You are always meant to stay, here, as close to me as possible."

I smile and crawl in next to him. He wraps his arms around me, we sit close together and lean back against the pane of the partially closed window. I breathe in the smell of his Ivory soap.

"They want to move. We're moving." He blurts it like a confession.

My mind races. He's leaving? When? I'm not ready. It seems like forever before I squeak back, "Where?"

"It won't matter how far apart we are, you know, we love each other, you're my girl." His voice is rushed, he fiddles with something in his hand and hunches forward to look into my eyes.

"Here Doris, will you be my girl and wait for me?" He pushes his class ring into my palm, it feels cold and heavy.

"But where are you going?" I ask again, with a firmer voice but more panic.

"Don't worry, it'll be fine. We can write and telephone..." He tries to bring me toward him, I pull away, I squeeze the ring tight in my fist.

"Write? What? Paul, you're confusing me. Just tell me what is happening!" My insides twist. Oh, god, he's leaving me. I lean into him with my eyes shut and rest my head on his shoulder.

"Indianapolis... we are moving to Indiana." He says this with such exasperation that he flings his body, and mine, back against the window behind us.

This proves too much for the single pane of glass and it's slight wood frame. We fall backwards, in each other's arms, landing hard on the bedroom floor. Stunned, I can't catch my breath before I see the door fly open and four slipper clad feet stop inches from my face.

Glass is everywhere, I look from the feet to Paul and see his wide eyed panic. I avoid looking up at his parents. I hear his mother's measured voice.

"Paul? Doris? You two are..." she trails off here, trying to keep her composure.

I attempt to maneuver myself into an upright position without touching Paul or the shards of glass. I realize there is no graceful way to do this, so I forgo grace for speed and scramble to my feet.

The next second, I stand face to face with his mother and I wonder what the hurry was. Paul takes his time getting up, stopping to brush glass from his hair, prolonging the awkwardness of the moment.

His mother is not actually intimidating in looks but being my boyfriend's mother makes her so. She has Paul's large green eyes, her hair is light brown and pinned respectably. His father is shorter than me but is intimidating with his precise side part and large severe eyebrows.

"Mom, I'm sorry," Paul starts. I'm relieved he was able to speak first. I still can't find anything appropriate to say. I do my best to look remorseful instead of mortified and keep quiet.

"Paul, I don't understand what's going on here, where did Doris come from? What are you two doing?"

His mother's voice climbs higher in pitch as her imagination runs amok with the possibilities.

"Oh, you kids, do I even want to know?"

"Mom, no, look, I asked Doris to come here tonight. We were sitting on the roof and the window broke. I just wanted to talk to her. That's all, really." He looks at me and I continue to wear my remorseful face, only peeking at her from the corner of my eyes.

I feel warm, then lightheaded. I reach out and grab Paul's arm.

"Oh my Jesus, Doris you're bleeding, sit down dear," his mother leads me by the shoulders to Paul's bed.

"Greg, go get some towels and ice." She waves off Paul's father.

He returns quickly with bandages, ice and a glass of water.

Paul's mother gently dabs my face and applies a small bandage. I sip the water and find the courage to whisper a thank you, although I'm not sure anyone heard it. Paul looks at me with pleading eyes, but I don't know what he wants.

"Paul, we're going to bring Doris home," his dad announces. "And you are going to explain to this young lady's father what happened here. We will discuss it further tomorrow." The tone of his proclamation lets us know it's not negotiable. He makes a motion with his head that commands us to follow him downstairs.

I want to protest but I'm not sure how. We ride in silence for the few blocks drive to my house. My anxiety builds with each passing driveway. My father won't be home when we get there, my mother will be mortified at being caught asleep while I've apparently been running the streets.

When we pull up to the curb in front of my house, the windows are dark, it's a school night and everyone else is asleep. I see curtains move in the neighbor's window and I know this will be discussed by more families than ours in the morning. I find a single thread of courage and make a weak attempt to deter the plan.

"My father is out of town and my mother's asleep, I can have her call you in the morning sir, really."

"Doris, I cannot, in good conscience drop you off in the dark, on the curb with you bleeding and looking assaulted. My goodness, what would that make me."

He's right and I know it. I get out of the car and shut the door as quietly as possible. The three of us march up the walk with me in the lead. At the door, I knock, which is weird because it's my house, but I'm not sure how else to warn my mother. The porch light flips on and there's rustling inside. She first peeks through the window and signals us to wait a minute, I assume she's straightening herself up.

My heart starts to race. Dread, shame and a million other emotions well up inside me. My mother is never going to let me hear the end of this.

Will I get to see Paul again? I want to look at him, I need him to say it'll be alright but I can't make myself turn around.

The doorknob jiggles as she unlocks it. I'm sweating, my heart pounds louder and louder. When the door finally opens, there is a mix of confusion and alarm on her face. I try to say something but instead I put my head in my hands and cry.

#

(July 1957)

It's hot, even in the shade of the maple tree in Paul's front yard. A small trail of sweat creeps down my spine and I hope it doesn't show through my light cotton dress.

Paul helps his parents put the last few items for their drive to Indianapolis into the car. He wanted me to be here to make sure we saw each other up to his very last second in Ypsilanti.

"I guess that's it." He walks over and sits next to me in the shade.

"I guess so." I fiddle with the lace on my saddle shoe.

"Look at me, Doris." He touches my chin with his finger so I have to look up into his green eyes. "It's only a year right? I'll start college down there and then we'll work something out. Just give it some time."

I nod, we don't have a real plan for how this is supposed to work.

Paul's parents want him to go to college, Paul doesn't seem to know what he wants. I don't know what to expect, it feels unfinished.

"Here," he digs in his pocket and pulls out his class ring. "I found it in my room when we were moving stuff. You must have dropped it after, you know, we fell."

I touch the scab on my head and Paul starts to laugh. "I still can't believe that happened. I've never seen my Mom so bent out of shape."

"It's not funny!" I give him a playful slap, he takes my hand and kisses it. With an exasperated look I shake my head. "Your parents hate me now and my mom keeps peeking into my room at all hours to see if I've snuck out!"

"So do you still want my ring?" He asks with a sly smile.

"Of course."

He turns my hand over, drops the ring into my palm and closes my hand around it. This time it feels warm.

We brave a gentle goodbye kiss, both of us lean forward but only our lips touch.

His mom slams the car door and starts the engine. He looks deep into my eyes, then brings my closed hand to my chest. "Keep it close, okay?"

"Right here." I pat the space over my heart.

"Bye Doris." He gets up and walks backward until he gets to the car and hops in.

Bye, I think to myself but the tightness in my throat traps the word inside. Tears in my eyes blur the vision of Paul through the backseat window.

#

2

(Present)

The thumping is exhilarating, faster and faster the rhythm pounds in my ears like a heartbeat.

Who's heartbeat?

I open my eyes, it's my own heartbeat.

I feel odd, panicky and lightheaded.

I try to sit up but I'm so heavy. I try to move my arm but I only knock some books from the side table. One of my legs falls from the bed.

I change my mind. I don't want to get up. I try to stay in the bed but it's too late, I start to slide.

I think I let out a sound. I'm on the floor.

I see feet. I hear yelling. They lift me up.

There's Kay. I try to touch her, she looks scared. I cannot reach her.

I turn my head and go to sleep.

#

Flickering lights and far away voices awaken me. I attempt to sit up and find it takes more effort than I can gather. I stir and the blurred group at the foot of my bed disperses until only one figure remains. He comes closer into focus. It's Scott.

"Baby," I whisper, and reach toward him.

"No, not your baby, do you remember me?" Scott asks.

"Scott?" I say and reach again, but he doesn't take my hand.

"No Doris, not Scott. I wanted to see you, we have to talk," he says.

I stare into his face, searching the creases and grey hair for a clue. My heart flutters. I know this man. I love this man?

"Paul? ...Carl? ...You're not Scott?" I'm a little desperate.

The man's face lights up then saddens again. He swallows hard.

"I guess it doesn't really matter," he says more to himself than to me. He looks disappointed. My heart aches.

"I know you," I say emphatically and put my hand to my chest.

"You do, don't worry. It's not important." He sits next to me on the bed and brushes a piece of hair from my forehead.

I feel loved. I do love this man. I take his hand and kiss it.

The corners of his mouth twitch, again he swallows and clears his throat.

"Doris, I don't know if you'll remember this. I just want to be honest with you at least once, even though everyone says it will just worry you for no reason. Okay?"

I have no idea what he's talking about but I nod because I can tell he needs me to.

"I've been so lonely these past years. All I've wanted was you, but I can't have you. You have to know that I have loved you and still love you. If things would have gone differently it would have been us growing old together. But I just couldn't be alone anymore, do you know what I mean?"

Again I nod. This man loves me. A tear escapes from his eye and rolls slowly down his cheek. I reach up and wipe it away.

"Please, don't cry. It's okay," I bring his hand to my lips again.

More tears come. I wish I could sit up and kiss him but I'm stuck, weighted down.

I put my hands on his shoulders and try to pull him towards me. He's stiff and rigid. I close my eyes and pucker my lips up toward him. I feel him shudder, he crumples into me, curling his head into my chest.

My lips, left waiting, find the top of his head. His clean earthy scent fills my nose and it's comforting.

"I miss you. I miss you." he whispers over and over.

I smooth his thick grey hair. "I miss you too." I feel like I mean it.

He pulls away, wipes his face before he stands, then leans over and kisses me on the forehead. I hear him inhale deeply as he lingers. He squeezes my hand and whispers hoarsely, "Goodbye, Doris."

I can't reply before he retreats into a silhouette in the doorway.

There is a heaviness in my chest.

"Goodbye." I hear myself whisper to the empty room.

A nurse comes in just seconds later. I ask her if she knew my visitor. She gives a shrug and says, "A friend I suppose, I didn't get to talk to him. There was a woman with him too, but she didn't want to come in."

"Has anyone else been here?" The heaviness turns to fear. Am I alone?

Her eyes meet mine for a moment. "I don't think so ma'am, you only had the one visitor today but I've been off over the weekend."

My heart sinks, my mouth has gone dry. It's hard to take a breath.

"Am I alone?" I whisper.

She doesn't respond but takes a colorful afghan from a chair and spreads it over me. "There that's better," she says as if it answers my question.

She hands me a cup of water and a small cup of pills. There are more pills than I feel like there should be but I take them anyway. I don't trust myself today.

I lay back, pulling the afghan to my chin. I know that today is not a good day.

#

My stomach rumbles, I peek through my eyelids at the fluorescent lights above. To my right a woman reads a craft magazine with a ball of yarn on the front. I cough a little and put a shaky hand to my chest.

"Mom?" the woman chirps, her face becomes clear.

"Suzy." My voice is raspy and I give another little cough.

I smile at her.

She smiles too.

"Thirsty?" She grabs a styrofoam cup from the side table and gives me a sip. She kisses my head then pulls her chair closer.

"And hungry." I nod at her.

"It's on its way. The nurse just left and said they'll bring lunch in soon."

I feel good. I know I'm in a hospital, and who I'm with, although I don't know why I'm here. The clarity energizes me, I want to talk. The machine monitoring my blood pressure shows its increase. Suzy frowns.

"Mother, relax, don't get too excited."

"How's work?" It's not exactly what I want to know but it's what comes out.

She smiles. "Still working on another ADHD drug. It is formulated more specifically for a child's brain but it's hard to get to human trials."

Suzy is smart, so smart. It used to scare me when she was a kid. She always did everything on her own, her own way.

"But that's boring stuff. Do you know why you're here?" She continues without waiting for my reply. "You had *another* UTI. They said your blood pressure was elevated and the UTI had gone septic. Should I worry about Kay and how they care for you at the home?" She takes my hand, concern hangs across her brow.

"I don't think anyone is doing anything wrong. I guess I forget to go, or wipe or something." I can't say if this is true but I don't want to get anyone in trouble. I think about the word home and try to remember where I live. Only images of my childhood home flash through my mind.

"I think we'll have Kay start to log your liquid intake and urine output in a journal." She taps on her phone screen. "I'll set it up online, so Scott and I can check it too."

She looks pleased with herself but I feel a little irritated.

"I said it's fine honey, don't worry. Just talk to me now. Tell me about the kids."

She nods but finishes a minute or two of poking at her phone before she looks at me. It's obvious my bathroom habits will soon be public knowledge, regardless of how I feel about it.

She turns her phone around and shows me a picture of a fat, adorable toddler dressed in blue pajamas. He holds a chalkboard that says "Future big brother."

"This is your great grandson Sawyer! Melissa is going to have another baby soon and we are so excited! Can you believe I'll be the grandma of two grandkids!"

Suzy looks so proud. I can't help but smile with her. "I'm a great grandmother?" I ask mostly to myself.

Suzy laughs and holds my hand. I feel tired so I lean my head into my pillow and stare at my beautiful, smiling daughter. I drift off with an empty stomach and a full heart.

#

I stop abruptly at the end of the hallway. The door looks familiar, I reach out to inspect the beveled plaque with my fingers. D - O - R ...

My halt causes someone behind me to give me a nudge. A dark arm snakes around me to grab the door handle. I side step to see that the arm belongs to a short dark skinned man carrying two large travel bags. He gives me a bright smile and pushes the door open.

"After you Ms. Doris."

The smell of Lysol wafts over us as we enter the small bright room. It has a cozy feel in spite of its neatness and the sterile smell.

"Is it good to be back in your own room, Ms. Doris?" The mans' accent is strong although I can't place it.

"Well, I suppose it will do." I'm not sure this is my room but he seems very confident so I agree. "I'll only have to stay here a little while but thanks for taking me in."

He gives me a slightly confused look and drops the bags on the recliner.

"Look here, your plant has been missing you. I watered it while you were in the hospital but still it droops without you."

I look blankly at the plant. It means nothing to me, so I shrug.

I think about his words as I look around the room, I was in the hospital? Anxiety starts to creep in, I take a deep breath.

"So what was your name again? I always have trouble with names. I swear I would forget my own sometimes."

The young man throws his head back and laughs harder than I would expect at my lame humor.

"Gavin ma'am, I work here. I have known you for many months now Ms. Doris. We're old friends." His funny accent makes the words sound like music, he sticks out his hand and I shake it. His smile soothes the anxiety that had started in my chest.

This time I chuckle, "If you say so, but you're too young to be anyone's old friend."

I wander to the bed and feel the soft afghan at its foot. I trace the colorful chevron pattern with my finger. Up and down they go with so many colors.

A loose stitch catches my eye so I pull it and it gets longer. I pull again and it continues to grow. There is a gratification as I watch the thread being released from the order of the blanket. I pull my arm high above my head and the rainbow string does not resist.

"Ms. Doris, stop. You love that blanket. You're going to ruin it." Gavin grabs the yarn and tugs it from my hand.

"No, I don't." I glare at him. "Let me have that back."

I grab at the thread and he quickly gathers up the blanket.

"Fine then, I'll put this up so it is out of the way." He puts the bundle in the closet then busies himself with emptying the bags from the recliner.

"Are you tired or would you like to watch TV?" He tries to give me a smile but I'm still annoyed at him.

I defiantly look away and plop down on the bed. It's soft and welcoming, I suddenly am very tired. I lay back and try to scoot myself up the bed but I can't get anywhere. I seem to be stuck, I curl on my side to face the wall.

"Let me take your shoes now Ma'am." I feel Gavin remove the shoes from my feet, then he pushes a pillow under my head. "Are you comfortable?"

I nod stubbornly even though I am not, at all, comfortable.

#

(September 1957)

From my stool in the corner of the fabric shop, I hear the voices of two women at the counter begin to raise. I tie off the end of a colorful chevron afghan for a window display.

My mother is at the counter discussing my working hours with Mrs. Atkins, who owns the shop. I picked up a few days here over the summer to help my family out and Mrs. Atkins would like me to continue through the school year.

"Connie," says Mrs. Atkins to my mother, "I know her senior year is a special time but Doris is just such a help around here, if you would let her work on Saturdays at least..."

I hope I'm allowed to continue working here. Since Paul left I've realized how few friends I have.

He and I exchange letters every week or so, and the time I tried to call him it was hard to hear since our neighbors on the party line kept picking up the phone. It wasn't really worth the high price of the call. I've saved a bit of money from every payday for a bus fare to visit him.

The chimes on the front door ring as a young man enters the store. He's tall with large shoulders and black hair combed back but tousled. His jeans slouch over his boots and the sleeves of his t-shirt are tight around his biceps, he reminds me of a dark James Dean.

"Carl! My goodness, could you please get dressed before you come to the store, where is your shirt!" Mrs. Atkins screeches as she hurries towards her son.

"Mom really, be cool. It's OK, I got a shirt in the car." Carl smirks and pecks her on the cheek.

He looks over at me and winks. I feel my face turn red and look back at my work.

Ugh, I can't believe he caught me staring, again.

My face gets redder as I remember last week when he came to the shop on a motorcycle and I'm fairly certain my mouth was actually open as I stared at him through the front window. I thought Mrs. Atkins was going to faint that day.

"Doris, right?" I look up to find Carl standing very close to me. All I can do is nod.

Carl cracks a huge smile and his amusement at my discomfort makes me irritated with him.

"So I go back to school next week and it would be a shame if we didn't get to know each other a little bit." He leans casually against the wall.

"Really, and why's that" I look back down at my work, surprised at my own sauciness.

He shuffles his feet and looks toward the door. I feel a little bad about my remark.

"Well, I uh, always see you here and thought maybe you might want to get out and have a little fun but, hey," he starts to back away. I find I don't want him to go.

"I wouldn't mind, but I have a boyfriend, so it would just be for fun, you know."

He looks relieved and the smile creeps back across his face.

"A boyfriend huh? Must be serious, but it's cool, we can just go out, get a bite. Everyone's gotta eat. How about I meet you here after closing today?"

"Cool. Okay."

Suddenly, I'm acutely aware of my mother's presence. She watches us from the checkout counter and doesn't look pleased.

Mrs. Atkins, on the other hand, is beaming.

"Doris, I don't think tonight's a good night. I need your help at home." My mother gives Carl a piercing look, and marches out the door before I can respond.

I look at Mrs. Atkins, who frowns at the swinging door from her post behind the counter. She huffs and hurries herself to the back of the store.

I'm left with Carl and his smirk, it's the one he usually wears when his mother chastises him.

"So are we still on?" he asks almost like a challenge.

"Everyone has to eat right?" I reply although my voice is quieter than I wanted.

"Cool." He says and saunters to the door, the chimes above

it announcing his departure.

My hands shake as I spin Paul's class ring on its chain around my neck.

#

(November 1957)

"Doris, will you take your brother to the library tonight?" My mother yells through the doorway down the hall where I see her trying to shake my father awake.

We have a car now so we don't have to walk everywhere in the cold Michigan fall. I usually drive so I can drop my father off at work then get us to school. I love to drive except that getting my dad to the car on time is usually near impossible.

"Come bring a wet rag for your father, we have to get him up, he can't miss work again."

I grab a washcloth, run it under the faucet and head to their bedroom. "Here," I say and thrust the dripping cloth toward her.

She takes it and dabs my father's face, he mumbles and bats her hand away. She rolls the washcloth up and puts it on his forehead.

"I'm meeting Carl after work today so can David walk home?" I try to slip quickly back to my room after this comment because I know what comes next.

"No, he does not need to walk home, *you* can bring him home, and it's a school night!" I hear her follow me down the hall.

She stands in my room with her eyebrows almost in her hairline. "You shouldn't mess around with Carl.

What would Paul think about this?"

"I don't know, mother, I haven't asked him. Carl and I are friends."

"Good girls don't need to be friends with boys, and you'll ruin your chances with Paul. Word gets around you know."

"Yes, I know, I've heard enough words from this town. Which is why I don't plan to stay in it. I need to get out and see what other places have to say."

"You aren't answering the question, what about Paul?" She blocks the doorway as I try to get by.

"Ugh, Mom, I'm going to be late!"

"Paul is fine. He is hours away, probably making all sorts of new *friends*. I haven't seen him in months. Plus, I gave you guys most of my bus fare money so who knows when I'll get to see him again!"

I duck by her to try to get to the bathroom but my father beats me inside and it could be forever before he emerges.

"Seriously," I groan, and turn on her. "I can't just sit in my room and wait for the mail! You did it the 'right' way and married Dad before you even got out of high school. "And this," I say loudly and point at the bathroom door, "is not what I want."

"Doris Irene McArthur," my mother grabs my arm, half drags me back to my bedroom and slams the door.

"You will not talk to me like that and you'll not bring your father into this. I'm just telling you, you better watch out. Life will teach you some lessons young lady. I'm trying to keep you from learning the hard way."

She's red faced, her hair flies around her as she leans in and points at me. "You have no idea what life can do to a person."

We hear the bathroom door open and my father muttering to himself as he stomps down the stairs. My mother gives me a meaningful look.

"Well, I know what it does around here." I smirk and roll my eyes towards the door.

She turns slightly then slaps me hard across the face. "You need to learn when to stop."

#

(December 1957)

Carl never picks me up from my house, we usually meet somewhere in town, even if it's just to go somewhere else together.

We haven't talked about it but I think we both agree that having him come to my house would be uncomfortable at best. For me, it somehow feels less like a date this way and we both avoid the glare from my mother.

Tonight, we met at the fabric shop and took his car into Ann Arbor. "The Parrot" is noisy and crowded with college students but we find an open booth near the door. I order a coffee because I think it makes me seem older then load it with sugar when it arrives.

"Hey, are you alright? You seem quiet?"

"Yeah, I just feel weird because I didn't tell my parents I was leaving Ypsi." It's a partial truth. I tear off a piece of the white paper napkin and roll it into a ball.

Carl leans forward over the small table to catch my eye, the woodsy scent of his aftershave punctuates his nearness.

"Relax, doll." He gives me his trademark smirk. "Did they ask?"

I surrender a small smile. "No, but my mother won't make eye contact with me when she knows I'm meeting up with you. She thinks you're "distracting" me." I ball another piece of napkin.

Carls' smirk spreads into a full mischievous grin, "and from what will I distract you, or dare I not know?"

"Come on, you already know... school and ...well, Paul." I look at my coffee when I say Paul's name.

Carl continues to tease me, "Ah, of course the respectable Paul. Did you tell her that my dark charms are no match for the square virtues of her hero?"

"Really, be nice," I blush, and smooth my skirt over my knees.

"I have no problem with Paul, don't worry. I remember him from school. He was a nice kid. Everybody liked Paul."

Carl reaches across the table and runs his finger along the back of my hand as it clutches my coffee cup. The connection sends a current up my arm and my heart races. I look up, our eyes meet.

"The only problem is that I like you more."

I'm hot all over. I feel petrified but I like it. This is so different than what it's like with Paul.

Where everything with Paul is comfortable and expected, everything with Carl is edgy and unpredictable.

I finally exhale, "Will you stop mocking me."

Thankfully, we are interrupted by two of Carl's rather dramatic looking friends.

One wears a turtleneck and light blonde fuzz on his chin while the other wears a dark grey striped sweater with glasses that look much too small.

"Hey, Carl man! How's it goin'?" Small Glasses asks, looking me over.

I pull my ponytail over my shoulder and curl it around my finger. I wish I would have at least worn my hair down so I might pass for older.

"Just getting a bite here with a *friend* from back home, you know." He raises his eyebrows and accentuates the word friend in a way that makes it seem like he does not mean friend at all.

"This is Doris." He gives me a wink.

"Cool, hey Doris," Small Glasses smiles.

Suddenly a voluptuous brunette bounces into the booth shoving me toward the window.

"Frankie," the girl squeals at Small Glasses, "We're hitching to Berkeley over Christmas, you should totally come!"

Fankie rolls his eyes away from the bouncy girl and gives Carl a look. "Donna, I have a car, I don't need to hitchhike. Actually, would you like a ride?".

Donna deflates and pouts "Well that doesn't sound like fun."

She turns, like she just noticed I was there.

"Hi, are you Carl's girl?"

I blink and try to come up with a reply. "Uhh, no, I'm a friend. I think…"

"You think? Ha! She's a riot." Donna exclaims then bounds off to another group just entering the café.

I look at Carl and he chuckles to himself. "You'll be alright Doris. These guys are just all jazzed up on Coca-Cola. They can be a little much. Let's get you home."

#

3

(January 1958)

The bus ride to see Paul has taken twice as long as expected because of the January snow in Indiana. I know his mother won't be happy, since I was supposed to arrive 4 hours ago and it's almost 9 p.m.

It's Paul's parents 20th anniversary dinner and I hope I haven't ruined it for him. I planned to stay with a neighbor of theirs who has an extra room but I'm not sure what will happen at this late hour. The trip is almost a wasted one since my bus leaves at noon tomorrow and I'm sure we will be expected at church.

When we finally pull into the station, I find Paul under the overhang. He rushes to grab my bag and we hurry back to his car through the drifting snow.

When we get in he takes my hand, leans over and kisses me softly. He is warm but the snowflakes are cold melting on his lips.

"Oh Doris, I'm so glad you made it. This storm is crazy."

Paul looks sweet with his red cheeks and grey knit hat.

"Tell me your folks aren't too mad, did you get to the dinner?" I ask with a grimace.

"Yeah, it's alright, I snuck out before dessert but they knew what was going on. They can't blame you for the weather!"

Paul holds my cold cheeks in his warm hands and we kiss, slowly, for a long time.

"I have to say something important," he says when we pull apart. "I can't wait until tomorrow because I don't know when we'll get to be alone again."

I get a tingle in my stomach and wonder if this will be a proposal. Do I want to spend the rest of my life with Paul? I'm not sure I'm ready.

Paul takes off his hat and fidgets with it before he speaks.

"It didn't seem right to tell you in a letter and we've only been able to talk on the phone the one time long distance..." He looks down and continues to fidget.

Excitement and fear build, he clears his throat before he continues.

"I joined the Army. I start boot camp in Georgia next week."

I don't realize I'm holding my breath, my words come out raspy and rushed.

"When did you decide this? What happened to college? I thought you were taking classes." I turn to the window.

This is not what I expected, he has never mentioned the Army.

"My Dad served in Germany, he thinks the military will be good for me, and I don't know what I'm doing in college. I feel like it's a waste of time."

He holds my hand again but I can't look at him. I pull it away to draw hearts on the fogged up windows.

"You keep getting further and further away from me, am I just supposed to wait for you to come back?"

"I love you Doris, I'll do whatever you want to do. You're my girl."

"What if you get hurt, what if you get sent somewhere and never come back? I'll graduate soon and be eighteen in a few months, just wait for me and we can go somewhere together." I plead with him, this is not part of the plan.

"Look at me," he lowers his voice and I turn toward him. "It's already set, they're expecting me. I just had to make a choice between another semester of classes and this. Maybe you can come with me, you can live on the base. Do you want to get married?"

His face looks earnest but unsure.

"Married? That's not a proposal, Paul. You don't even have a ring." I cross my arms and slide down into my seat.

No. This is not what I want, I don't want to be a military wife. I think of my parents.

Paul reaches over and touches my chin. I turn to look at him, his eyes are big and sorry. My heart aches. I lean in and kiss him. I know this is goodbye.

We continue to kiss with more and more urgency as headlights from passing cars flicker through the fogged windows. Kissing is easier than talking.

"Can we go somewhere quiet?" I'm hopeful he understands my meaning.

He pulls away and looks me in the eyes.

"Now?" A look of excitement and possibly fear hang on his face.

"Please," I whisper.

He drives us out of the city, silent in thoughts of what we're about to do.

We've come close so many times. On the roof, in his car this summer; we always stopped because we were sure we would have our time together in the future.

I can't imagine letting him go but I know we won't survive this separation. I can't end up like my mother. There's no reason to wait anymore, we're out of time. I need him close, I want to feel as close to him as possible. I love him. I want him to know how much.

We park behind a small school. The snow has stopped and the moon is bright. The swingsets glitter in the headlights.

He leaves the car running, Fats Domino's velvety voice croons Blueberry Hill through the radio.

I give him my best Brigitte Bardot come hither look and climb awkwardly into the back seat. Paul's eyes are wide in the rearview mirror, his hand trembles on the steering wheel.

"Well are you coming back here or what?" I ask trying to sound flirty but the crack in my voice gives it away.

Paul turns in his seat. His mouth twitches as he looks me over. His fingers drift to the top button of his stiff white shirt.

"Are you sure?" He asks undoing the button.

I nod.

Paul hastily removes his shirt and climbs eagerly into the back seat. A patch of golden hair peeks from the top of his undershirt. I watch it heave up and down with his breath as he hovers just inches away.

I tilt my chin up towards him, and hold his gaze. My tongue self consciously wets my lips.

With a short pause and a deep breath, he pulls me toward him. Our kisses turn from gentle to hard. Our teeth and lips bang together and I don't care. We don't pull away and giggle as we usually would.

He starts to unbutton my shirt quickly, when my bra is completely exposed he pauses staring from my chest to my face. Neither of us know exactly what to do, how do we cross this line?

I take his hand, I can feel it shake as much as my own. Doubt creeps in and I wonder why I'm doing this? Should I stop?

I press his hand up under my bra before I lose my nerve. A small groan escapes his lips. He pushes my bra up over my head and cups my breasts firmly in both hands. Slowly, timidly, he lowers his mouth to one of my nipples. It's my turn to groan as we slide down across the backseat.

He releases me to pull his t-shirt off and I get a partial glimpse of his lean body before we are pressed skin to skin.

An electric current sails through me, it reminds me of Carl. His face flashes through my mind and I quickly push it away.

I tug at Paul's belt and slide my hand over his zipper. I'm surprised at the hardness underneath. Paul sits up and struggles awkwardly with his pants.

I slide my skirt up my thighs and slowly unhook my stockings. Paul is mesmerized by each inch of revealed flesh. In the dark I see only the shadows of him exposed. I slide my underwear down and lie back on the leather seat. Arranging himself between my legs, he leans over me and whispers "okay?" I nod and close my eyes.

He pushes into me, at first with awkward difficulty, then we find a rhythm and glide together. It's gentle and not at all what I expected.

A few minutes later it's over. We look away as the other reassembles themselves in the darkness. A silence hangs between us too long after we are dressed.

Paul takes my hand and pulls me close. He kisses the top of my head and says, "Thank you, Doris."

I doubt that "you're welcome" is the appropriate response. We stay like this for a few minutes in silence before I pull away and respond with a kiss.

"Your parents are going to wonder where we are, you know." I say, anxious to leave.

We climb into the front seat and drive back toward the city. Out the window, tall buildings rise suddenly from the wide flat farmland that sprawls in either direction. I feel so far from what I know, even from Paul.

He doesn't notice the difference. He wears a goofy grin all the way to his neighborhood.

I look out the window and try to keep the tears from falling. I just want to go back home.

#

(April 1958)

The folded pages of Paul's letter flap gently in the breeze from my open bedroom window. It waves from the desk, cheery and expectant. He's almost done with his training in Georgia, he wants to know when I'm coming to see him after I graduate.

I haven't told him that I'm not his girl anymore, or that the visit to Indiana was the last I expected to see him.

I'm afraid to give him up. He is the first good, real and normal thing I ever had. But I've seen this all play out before. Girls wait for their hero to return from war or some overseas post, then he comes back changed and broken; or he doesn't come back at all.

They are stuck here alone, or with a man not at all like the boy they loved.

I think of my mother and father. We have one picture of our family from before my father left to go overseas. In it, my Dad waves at the camera with all his fingers and an easy smile. My mother sits close to him, pregnant with my brother David. I play on the floor in front of them. It all looks so normal and promising.

I barely remember the time he was gone. I do remember when he came home and how exciting that day was, and how I couldn't stop staring at his missing fingers.

No, I wouldn't be able to handle that with Paul. I will not be one of those girls, and I am not ending up with one of those guys.

I know Paul will be fine. I'm the one who has needed him to get through my life. It hurts a little to think of him moving on, realizing how easily I will be replaced with the type of girl Paul belongs with. I know my pain is hypocritical and it makes me more certain Paul can do better.

I sit and try to think of what to write back. He's written me three letters and I've written three responses, all ending our relationship. They each have only made it as far as the tiny trash can in the bathroom. I feel like I don't really want to do this, but I have to. This time I promise myself I will mail it.

Dear sweet Paul,

I am sorry it has taken me so long to write, I'm glad you like your training. I'm sure you look handsome in your uniform.

I've got to be honest, I'm not waiting for you. I have been seeing someone else. I do love you, and I know I'm hurting you but please know I can't help it. You're the best thing that has ever happened to me. I don't know what I would have done without you, you have given me so much.

I used to think that I needed you, that you made me good and that there was no "me" without you. But I have figured out over the last year how to be me without you, even though it's not easy.

It seems life continues to lead us apart. I'm graduating soon and I have to think about my future. I can't be with someone who isn't here. I just don't know how to be with you now that you're gone. And you know, I have already had one military man in my life, that's enough for me.

I'm sure you will find someone else soon, you are such a good person.

Please stay safe and goodbye.

I'm sorry.

With love,

Doris

I fold the letter neatly and tuck it into the envelope. I reach into the tray on my desk and retrieve Paul's ring. I slip it over my finger, kiss it, then take it off and put the ring in the envelope. I wipe a tear from my cheek, take a deep breath and head to the mailbox.

#

(Present)

My hands shake with excitement.

I dig through the drawers, I know I will find it soon. I put it here somewhere. There's so much stuff in these drawers though, it's in my way. I'll just take it out for now. Nope, not in the top drawer, I would never put it there anyway that's too predictable.

"Oh, Ma'am, oh, Doris, what are you doing?"

I turn and see the little man in the doorway.

"I'm looking for it and I know it's here somewhere, are you here to help?"

"Uh, yes ma'am," he says looking astounded by the mess of undergarments strewn around the room.

"What are we looking for Ms. Doris."

This is a good question so I ponder it for a moment. I see it in my head. What is it.....

"It's mine, and I want it. It's cold and green on the top," I point to my finger.

Gavin gives me a smile and says, "Is it a ring Ms. Doris, is that what you are looking for?"

I nod. Gavin takes my place digging in the dresser drawer.

The curtains are open and a pair of cardinals are at the feeder outside the window. They peck in the little tray, oblivious to my watching. A large blue jay lands abruptly at the top of the feeder. The brightly colored male cardinal flits away but the duller female startles only for a moment then returns to her perch at the feeder.

"So you think you put it in here?" says a voice from behind me.

"What?" I turn to see a little man about to open the bottom drawer of my dresser.

"You think you put your ring in the dresser Ma'am?"

"Why would I do that? I have my pajamas in that drawer. You get out of there anyway. You're making a mess," I point around the room at the clothing strewn about.

"Yes, right," says Gavin, he takes a deep breath before standing up. He looks at me for a moment and shrugs, "Can I take you to the living room? They're playing a game."

"Sure, I'll probably just watch, I don't like games." I take a step and my foot tangles in a thick white bra-strap. I unsuccessfully try to kick it off so Gavin bends down to set me free. He tosses the bra back on the floor near a small pile of silky white undergarments.

"Is someone going to clean this up?" I wonder out loud.

Gavin opens his mouth like he's going to say something then closes it and nods. He holds the door open for me. I pass by him with a smile and head down the hall.

#

I've found some letters from my family, they're probably wondering when I'm coming home. I'm definitely leaving today. I stuff them in my purse quickly before someone sees.

"Okay, Doris, let's get ready to go," A familiar woman with a dark floppy bun startles me when she pops her head in the door. "We're going holiday shopping!"

I don't return her enthusiasm. "No thanks, I need to go home, you can just drop me off." I say looking around for my shoes.

The woman's smile drops and she steps squarely in front of the door.

"Doris, hun, this is your home. You live here." She wags her finger toward the room.

"No," I sit on the bed to push on a pair of boots. "I live in Ypsilanti. Our house is just off Hamilton Street. I can show you."

The woman is quiet for a moment. Then walks over to a picture on the wall.

"If this isn't your home then why would we have this picture of you hanging here? And those pictures over there are of your kids." She points to a cluster of frames on the opposite wall.

"I don't know about all that, but I don't live here and I'd like to go home." I stand and sling my purse over my shoulder. "It's a small grey house, it has an iron fence and gate. The front porch screen is broken…"

I can visualize all the details, I can't wait to go home and sleep in my own bed.

"I can't promise to take you home Doris, but we can go out today, alright?" the woman looks a little concerned or maybe annoyed, I can't tell.

"Well alright, then maybe I can call a cab or my mom. She'll come get me. Where is this place?" I head towards the door but the woman doesn't move.

"This place is in Ann Arbor and you live here Doris. Why don't you just relax today. You can sit in your recliner and I can turn on the game show channel?"

"No, I want to go home! Now please move so I can make a call." I try to get around her but she blocks me in. Her persistence frightens me. Why won't she let me leave, this is not my home.

"Doris, we can't do this right now." A horn honks from outside. "Everyone else is already in the van, I can stay with you if you don't want to go."

Her voice is strained but calm. She tilts her head to keep eye contact with me as I look down at her bright white tennis shoes. I just want to get past her.

"I want to go." I say quietly.

"Okay, are you going to be good?" She leans down to make

sure I look at her face. She has her eyebrows raised high, causing the skin between her brow and hairline to fold itself into thick neat rows. I nod and stare at the folds until she turns around to lead the way.

As we walk, I watch my feet and the black puffy boots I have on remind me of something an astronaut would wear. I'm distracted thinking about astronauts as we make our way out the door.

Outside the chill takes my breath away, the air smells fresh and cold. When we get to the van, a large heavy door slides open. There is a cheerful looking black driver up front. Two old women sit directly behind him on the first bench and I make out the shadow of a man in the far back seat.

"Let me help you in." The woman next to me shoves a pudgy hand toward me.

One of the women in the front wears a bright green sweater and a Santa style hat. "Are we going to the mall? I need to find a toy store." She yells out the door.

"No, I'm going home." I answer her, remembering my mission. I don't take the woman's hand and turn to look her in the eye. "Right? This bus is taking me home?"

She gives the driver a meaningful look and he turns off the van.

"Why don't we go back inside for a bit Doris. I think we forgot something." She gives me an insincere smile and nods a lot.

Something about her demeanor isn't right. The van door starts to close and there is a soft beeping sound. She reaches towards me.

"No!" I shout and stomp my boot on the slushy drive. "I want to go home! Why won't you take me home!"

"I've had enough of this, I'm going home now!" I walk down the driveway toward the street.

The woman hurries to stay beside me. "Doris, you need to stay here. You can't walk home. It's too far."

"I don't care. I just want to go home, I can walk. Which way is Ypsi?" I look up and down the street. The sidewalks are clear with high piles of snow alongside them. The road is three lanes and all the homes are situated together snugly. Nothing looks familiar.

"Look Doris, I have my phone right here." She takes a small device from her pocket. "Let me call and get you a ride okay?"

I take a few more steps and slide a little on the slush where the driveway meets the sidewalk. I eye her suspiciously as she holds the phone and points to it with her eyebrows high, the heavy folded skin returning and her head nodding.

"Just let me get you a ride, then you can go home safely. Besides, you don't have all your stuff." She points to the purse on my shoulder and the envelopes sticking out of it.

"You left a bag of your clothes and shoes in the house." She takes a couple steps backwards. I notice a small black man standing near the back of the van with his arms folded.

"I left my stuff inside?" I say, in an attempt to make sense of her words and the scene at hand. I know I'm angry but the reason is sliding away from me. I'm not sure where this is going.

"Yes, let's go in, you can wait inside while I make the call." The woman speaks slowly as she shakes the phone at me, her head continues to bob up and down.

I don't speak but start to walk toward the house. I don't trust her but I'm not sure what else to do.

When we get inside she leads me down the hall to a familiar room.

"Well here it is, home sweet home," she says and goes over to turn on the T.V.

"No, this is not my home." I say emphatically, the feeling and phrase both familiar.

"I'll put the game show channel on for you honey, why don't you take off your coat and boots and have a seat." She waves her hand at the recliner positioned directly in front of the television and reaches for my purse. I yank it away from her.

"But I want to go home." The words echo in my head.

"I can't do this today, Doris. I'm sorry." The woman says with a heavy sigh as she slips into the hallway and shuts the door behind her.

I grab at the handle but it won't turn, I'm locked in.

"Noooooo!" I say and slap the door. It hurts my hand. I walk to the bed and sit down. I throw the purse across the room, envelopes and papers scatter everywhere.

"But I want to go home." I start to cry.

#

4

When Carl talks passionately his dark eyes are bright and animated, I can't help but want to be excited with him. His enthusiasm always has that effect on me.

"Doris, this is going to be great. There will be thousands of students there, demanding integration in schools...."

I nod along. I find myself in love with his drive to help others, and his willingness to defy everyone for what is right. For all his attempts to rebel, he is really very sensitive and caring.

I don't always understand what he and his friends are excited about. Sometimes it's the south, sometimes it's the Russians, sometimes it's everybody. I've figured out there are enough strong opinions in the group that I can usually just smile along without anyone needing me to add anything.

"...oh, man, I wish you were coming. Babe, I'm going to miss you like mad. You do know you're missing something big right?"

"Carl, my mom would flip if I left with you guys. She gets worked up enough with me coming to Ann Arbor, nevermind taking a van to Washington, D.C."

"Well, you know you're almost an adult, you can do what you want Doris."

"That's easy for you to say, you guys have your own place. I'll live with my parents until I'm married." I plop down on the couch in the living room of Carl's apartment.

My mother thinks it's scandalous that I visit him here but I decided to stop telling her and she's stopped asking. The room is decorated with sculptures that Carl has made and other art he and his roommates have collected. Books by Whitman and Kerouac, as well as their college textbooks, are strewn about mixed with records and ashtrays filled with cigarette butts.

Carl is lucky, his mother pays for his school and pays his rent so he easily gets by selling art and doing odd jobs. The two other boys he lives with are from up north, they both have to hold jobs while they go to school.

"Sounds horrible," Carl kneels in front of me with exaggerated sympathy. "Here, why don't you let me help you feel better."

He leans in with a long, slow kiss, nibbling my bottom lip. I lean back on the couch, he crawls up next to me, almost on top of me. He pulls me close, his body is solid, his hips grind into mine.

"Come to my room?" It sounds like both a question and a command.

I draw my breath. I have denied Carl for months, he never pushes me but I worry about the older girls that run in his crowd.

I know they do it. I hear plenty of them talk about it when we hang out. Carl never mentions other girls, yet I can't help but take their presence as a threat. Especially those riding down south on this trip.

Out of both yearning and fear I hear myself whisper, "yes."

"Okay?" He looks startled, then a smile creeps across his face,"Are you sure? You usually say no."

I push him off me and walk backwards toward his room. "Well, I guess I will just go in by myself then."

"I'll be damned woman, you are full of surprises."

#

(December 1958)

Carl came back from the march a few weeks ago with a ton of stories. Coretta King spoke in place of her husband and Carl went on and on about the stabbing of Martin Luther King, Jr. There are rumors of another March in Washington next year, Carl and his friends have plans to recruit more people to go.

"You have to come next year, I'll kidnap you and take you against your will, I swear. If you could just see it, then you would know how important it is. People around here just don't know, they haven't seen the courage, or the need, the Negroes have. The people here are blind."

"It sounds amazing Carl. Believe me, I can't wait to get out of this town."

The winter weather has made it more difficult for me to take the car to Ann Arbor, so we've started to meet at the Chick Inn diner in Ypsi. My mother still doesn't approve of Carl but she's been distracted trying to make ends meet and covering for my father. He stopped going to work weeks ago and has started disappearing for longer stretches of time.

I watch Carl, smoking coolly at the table. He doesn't have the worries I do. He really thinks he's going to do great things, make the world better. He's not just surviving, he is living.

I envy and love that in him. When we're together I'm sprinkled with a little of the magic that seems to follow him. I hope he'll really take me with him. For me he's a buoy in the reality I have been drowning in my whole life. I just hope I can hold on.

"What are you smiling at Doll?" Carl winks at me and blows a smoke ring.

"Just thinking about saving the world with you." I blush, immediately regretting my flippant honesty.

"Ha!" Carl's burst of laughter echoes through the small restaurant. A couple of waitresses look up at us. "You're a riot, Doris, and pretty too." He reaches over and touches my cheek.

I'm relieved he thinks I'm funny but I start to feel a little nauseous.

"Carl, I think I need to go home."

Carl looks disappointed. "I was hoping you would want to go hang out somewhere more romantic or something." He snubs out the cigarette in the tray on the table and blows the last of the smoke from his mouth.

I know what the "or something" means and we've only done "something" one other time since he's been back because the opportunity has been hard to come by. I consider the possibility for a moment but the rock in my stomach makes the decision for me. I just hope I can get back to the car without vomiting.

"No, I have a headache, I really need to go Carl." I look apologetically at him but stand to move him along quicker.

He lands a quick kiss before I escape into the car and drive away. Just before I get onto River St., I throw up on the side of the road.

No work for me tomorrow and I say a prayer of gratitude when I make it home without needing to make another stop.

#

(January 1959)

I've been standing outside Carl's apartment building for the last 10 minutes.

Through a cracked window I've listened to his downstairs neighbor play "Smoke Gets in Your Eyes" at least three times.

A break up song, maybe it's a sign.

Finally, through a combination of desperation and hypothermia, I get the nerve to march up the snow covered steps and knock. Carl pulls the door open so quickly it makes me wonder if he knew how long I had been standing outside.

"Holy cow it's cold!" I exclaim nervously, stomping into his apartment.

Carl takes my coat and brushes a few damp snowflakes from my hair, "Here let me warm you up." He wraps me in his arms and kisses me with a passion I can't return at the moment. He must credit my stiffness to the cold because he backs away and rubs my arms, "Man, you're shivering, come sit down."

He grabs a quilt from the back of a chair and I plop myself onto the low brown couch.

"Carl, I've got to tell you something." I blurt with my voice shaking.

"Okay." Carl sits next to me with innocent expectation. Not noticing my anxiety, he takes the time to spread the quilt over my lap. He has no idea I'm about to ruin our lives.

I start to cry. He reaches over to hold me but I push him away and scoot further along the couch.

"What's going on?" He touches my chin and tilts his head down to look at my face. "Are we splitting? Look at me doll, please, you're scaring me."

I've been thinking about this for days. I've debated about what to tell him and I've looked with my soul into all the options. In the end, I've decided I'm too scared to make any decisions without him.

I find my courage and look him in the eyes, "I think I'm pregnant."

He stands up quickly and takes a few long strides towards the door. I wonder if he's just going to walk out. It was one of the hundred scenarios that ran through my mind in the last few hours.

Suddenly he releases a loud laugh, he has tears in his eyes when he turns around. The tears and the smile give his eyes a maniacal glitter. I feel a little scared.

"Oh, Doris, oh babe. I thought I was losing you. I thought you were leaving me." He rushes back to the couch and wraps his arms around me. He tries to pull me into him but I have to be sure he heard me.

"Carl, I'm pregnant. Did you hear me?" He sits back on his knees and smiles at me.

This reaction was in none of the scenarios I rehearsed in my head.

"Yeah, it's okay. We'll get married. We'll be alright."

My mind is spinning. Why isn't he freaking out?

"So you're not mad at me?" I ask just to check that I'm not missing something.

"Of course not, I mean we knew this could happen and we did it anyway..."

For some reason this comes as another surprise to me.

I don't think I knew this could really happen, not to me and not from the two times we had sex. I guess I figured there was some protection for people who weren't ready for kids or a sort of beginner's luck grace period. I just didn't think about getting pregnant.

"Yeah, I guess." I say because I don't want to seem stupid.

Carl stands up and runs into his room. "Just wait there," he yells from out of sight.

He comes back after a minute with his hand behind his back and that same giddy grin on his face. "I just want to do this right," and he gets down on one knee in front of me.

My face flushes and I feel a mix of relief and nausea wash over me.

"Doris Irene McArthur, will you spend the rest of your life with me? Please be my wife." He holds out his hand and presents an earth toned clay ring. "It was going to be a piece of one of my sculptures, it was the best I could come up with on short notice. We can go and get something else once I get some money together…"

"No, Carl, it's sweet. And, yes, of course we should get married. I love you." I take the large ring and put it on my middle finger.

My insides shake. I'm grateful he isn't leaving me and that he'll stay and do the 'right' thing, but I'm not filled with the joy I thought this moment would bring. It's somehow not as fulfilling as I imagined. I still feel like me, still without answers, still a little trapped. Hot tears roll down my cold cheeks.

Carl scoops me up and carries me to his room. He lays me gently on the bed and wipes my wet cheeks. "I will take care of you Doris, and our baby. Don't worry."

"I'll try," I say, knowing Carl doesn't understand what he's signed up for.

#

(Present)

"Doris, you need to eat something else besides pickles, you're going to make yourself sick." Kay moves the tray of dill spears out of my reach.

"It makes me feel better, everything else makes me sick!" I reply emphatically and push my chair away from the table. I slouch down low in my seat, gingerly holding my stomach.

"Well, all that salt isn't good for you, try some bread if you aren't feeling well." Kay slides a roll onto my plate where the pickles had been. The bottom of the bread starts to yellow as it soaks up the remaining pickle juice.

"I'm not eating this." I flip over the roll with the tip of my finger. I stand quickly, my chair makes a loud screech on the linoleum and I bump the table with my hip. I lean on the shoulder of the grey haired lady next to me to steady myself. She yelps and pulls away.

"Get off me!" she screeches, swatting at my hand.

Kay looks at us both like we're naughty children. "Doris please don't touch Clara, you're startling her."

"Oh crap, Clara, I'm not hurting you, calm down." I sneer at Kay and stomp back to my room.

In my recliner, I find a bright afghan wrapped carefully around a pink bunny. It looks so sweet. I pick it up gently to sniff its head, it smells soft. I rock it, set it gingerly on the bed and return to my chair. A few minutes later the door creaks open and a bushy browed old man peeks into the room.

"Shhhhh…" I say as our eyes meet. I nod towards the bed. He smiles knowingly.

He tiptoes in and hands me a soggy, yellow stained napkin, then retreats into the hallway and closes the door. I open the parcel to find two pickle spears tucked inside. I take a couple bites, enjoying the salty taste. I fold the pickles back in their napkin, put them in my sweater pocket and wipe my hands on my slacks. I check on the baby, and carefully carry her back to the recliner with me.

A tune echoes in my mind and I start to hum. Soon the words come and I sing Smoke Gets in Your Eyes to the baby as I rock in the recliner.

#

At a picnic table under a canopy, I push blue baby bottle confetti around on a small white plate. The smoothness of the shiny plastic bottles sliding on the plate captivates me. I press on them with my fingers and they stick. Soon I have one stuck to the end of each finger.

A memory surfaces of Carl and I sticking blue confetti stars to each other and laughing. I smile to myself and try to place the image somewhere on the timeline in my mind. I'm lost in this thought when a light tap on my knee catches my attention.

"Grandma Doris, what're you doing?" I shake the memory to find a young girl staring up at me through dark curls.

"Well hello! How old are you sweetie?"

"Five, almost six in December." She says with pride.

"Well, you're old enough to learn a trick then aren't you?"

She nods and looks around like she's afraid to get caught. There is a paper cup with water in it sitting next to me.

"Okay, you sit here." I pat the seat in front of the paper

cup. She climbs up and looks at me expectantly.

"Watch this," I take a piece of confetti, a white swirl, and dip it into the water, then I stick it right to my forehead and smile.

The little girl's face bursts into a grin and she giggles, "Can I try?"

"Of course!" I push the plate of confetti toward her.

She selects a bottle, dips it in the cup and sticks it to her forehead. Her eyes cross as she tries to look where she stuck confetti. Now we're both giggling.

Soon we have covered our faces in little blue bottle confetti and whisper to each other at the table.

"Doris, what are you two doing?" A stern voice asks from behind us.

The little girl's eyes widen with a look somewhere between fright and mischievous. We turn in our seats to face a tall blonde woman with her hands on her hips.

"Momma, look what Grandma Doris taught me!" The girl says proudly as she adds another bottle to her face.

"Lana! My goodness you've made a mess! The front of your dress is all soaked!"

We look down at the wet spots that cover the front of her lavender sundress.

The woman purses her lips and breathes loudly through her nose. "Let me get something to get you cleaned up." She marches off toward the table covered with food.

"Oooh, mama does not like messes." Lana whispers with an impish grin.

"That's okay," I whisper, "messes are only for fun people." This makes Lana giggle until her mother returns with a tall man who looks at least 15 years older than her.

"Scott, you'll have to clean up your mother, I'll take care of Lana." The blonde shoves a towel at him and starts to dab at Lana's face.

"Mom, what is this?" Scott is trying to hide the same impish grin the little girl was wearing. The blonde shoots him a look and scowls.

"Just fooling around I guess. Your father taught me this trick. He thought it was funny. Carl loves to laugh, he's never afraid of messes." I shoot a look at the blonde wiping off Lana's dress. She rolls her eyes and wipes with more ferocity.

Scott's face softens and a good belly laugh escapes, he gives me a kiss on the cheek.

#

5

"You're one lucky girl Doris." My mother cannot resist another scornful lecture from her station in front of the sink.

"He could've left you here and gone off without you and you would have only yourself to blame. You had to run off to see him all the time. Now we'll have to figure this out so you're married before anyone can tell."

My mother is reacting exactly as I thought she would. Carl insisted on coming with me to tell her about our engagement, and the baby. She hugged Carl and assured him my father would be pleased.

"You have our blessing," She said with a smile, then sent him on his way, but I knew that wouldn't be the end of it.

"You've put your brother's reputation at risk as well you know. Poor David will have to put up with the whispers at school. What sort of family will people think we are." She scrubs a pan so furiously soapy water sloshes over the edge of the sink onto her feet.

"Sure mom, you don't need your whore daughter bringin' shame on the family after Dad has worked so hard to earn our great reputation."

She sends the pan splashing into the sink and rushes towards me, her face tight with anger. Her hand drips suds as she holds a wet shaky finger in my face and spats, "You watch your mouth. You don't get all high and mighty from your position young lady."

I push my chair back to get out from under her, standing to look her in the eye, "My position is as one of the people who bring food into this damn house, Mother. I help keep the lights on and sew David's clothes so no one knows what a failure you married. So yeah, I expect a little slack when I screw up. This whole family is screwed up. I get a turn too!"

I storm to my room and slam the door. Flopping onto my bed, I scream into my pillow. I can't wait to get out of this house. I promise myself, my kids will never have to take care of me the way I have had to take care of my family. This baby will get to have its own life and really live.

I roll to my back and stare at the ceiling. How will I ever get away from this town now? What are we going to do? None of this is what I wanted, or at least not how I wanted it.

Carl insists he can finish this semester at school and support us by selling his sculptures. God I hope he's right, I want things to be so different for this baby and for me. I sob until my pillow is soaked and I fall asleep to fantasies of a life with children who don't worry about their parents.

#

(February 1959)

Our wedding is quick and small. The whole thing feels off but Carl doesn't seem to notice. I hope it's just the pregnancy that makes the day feel like a chore. I can't help feeling like the ring is a tether to a life I'm not sure I want.

"My mom got us a room at the Highway Motel tonight, Mrs. Atkins." Carl says with a giddy smile.

I get goosebumps at the sound of my new name and I rub my hands on my arms. "I can't wait." I say truthfully, feeling so tired I think I could sleep anywhere.

We have spent the last few days preparing for the wedding, which consisted of a brief Friday morning ceremony in the church basement and a reception brunch. We have also begun to move both mine and Carl's things into his mother's house.

Carl's mother, Marylin, has been more than courteous and doting. I can't lift or move anything without her making a fuss. She doesn't seem to care that Carl and I aren't married, she is just so excited about her grandbaby.

Sometimes I wonder if this all reminds her of her own wedding and pregnancy. Carl says he's pretty sure his mother was pregnant for him at his their wedding. Marylin never talks about Carl's father, who died just after they opened the fabric shop. Carl has talked about him more since the pregnancy, always saying what a great dad he was.

Carl puts his arm around my waist and rubs the small of my back. The friction slowly untucks the thin satin blouse his mother made for me to wear today. I reach back and push the shirt further into my waistband. I kiss him on the cheek so he doesn't feel slighted when I move his hand away.

"You alright?"

"Yeah, just tired." I force a smile.

"We can get out of here soon, the cake's already been cut and it looks like people are starting to pack up."

I nod and move to peck him on the cheek again but he playfully turns his head so the kiss lands on his lips. He winks and walks toward a group of older ladies that surround his mother.

I close my eyes and take a deep breath, when I open them my mother has almost made her way from a corner table to my side.

"You look tired Doris."

I try to decide if this is concern or criticism, her crossed arm posture doesn't lend any helpful clues.

I start to reply but she reaches out and takes my hand. This surprise gesture stops my thoughts and makes me uneasy.

My mother looks pleadingly into my eyes, "Take care of yourself honey. Being a wife isn't always what you'd expect, and being a mother never is."

Her voice quivers and her eyes are teary. She blinks and looks down at our joined hands, she wraps her other hand tightly over mine.

Her lips move like she might say more, I squeeze her hand. "Yeah," is all I can get out over the tightness in my throat.

My father lumbers up behind her clapping his large hand on her thin shoulder. "Connie, lets git." He looks at me with loosely focused eyes and a slight sway in his stance, "You alright Doris?"

My mother lets go of my hand and shakes her head as if to free herself from the intimacy of the moment.

"She's fine, she's a married woman now. Let's go dear."

They both give me a nod, they stop to say goodbye to Marylin on their way out. I stare after them with an unfamiliar feeling of longing.

#

(Present)

I hurriedly finish my makeup before I start rummaging through the closet to find my dress. I need to leave soon and I don't know how it got so late.

The dark and cold make it hard for me to find what I'm looking for. I shush the hangers in the closet as they noisily bang against each other. I don't want them to wake Carl.

With my purse in hand, I tiptoe down the hall. My mother will be here to pick me up soon. I peek out the window and see headlights outside.

The door handle turns easily but doesn't open. I try the deadbolt and pull but the door only opens a few inches. I keep pulling but it won't budge. I hear a high pitched beeping.

"Wait mom, the door is stuck!" I yell through the gap.

The lights have disappeared from outside.

"No, mom, wait! I'm right here, the door is stuck, I'm coming!" I yank hard on the door but get nowhere, I jam my arm into the small opening.

"Wait!"

Suddenly the room is very bright.

"Doris! Oh, my lord! What are you doing?" A disheveled woman tries to yank me away from the door.

"Noooo, owwww" I yell, as my arm is pinched and twisted even further with her yanking. I try to pull the door again, it won't move, I start to sob.

"Doris, just calm down. Let's take your arm out of the door. Move slowly." She says eyeing my arm with concern.

"But I want to go to church. I missed my mom." I try to

peek through the crack again.

"I know honey," she answers, "but let's move your arm out of the door then we can find your mom."

It's cold and I want to pull my arm in but the movement seems too hard. "Help." I say quietly.

The woman gently moves my body over then slides my arm backwards out of the opening. My fingers are icy. She closes the door and looks at my arm.

"You're already getting a bruise here, honey." She points at my upper arm. "I guess I'll have to write up a report."

I nod and stare at her even though I'm not sure what she means. I assume I'm in some sort of trouble.

"Sorry." I whisper.

"Don't worry honey," she pets my hair and looks into my eyes. "You're okay."

I relax a little, I don't feel scared anymore but my body still shakes.

The woman's eyes wander over my face. "Let me get you a washcloth, it looks like you got into some makeup too."

She leaves and I touch my face then look at my hands. Black and pink smudges appear on my fingers.

"Don't rub it in, dear. Let me get it." She scrubs gently at my face with a warm cloth for then looks satisfied. It feels nice to have her there.

"I'll get the rest in the morning. Let's get you back in bed."

She holds my hand and leads me to a small room at the end of the hall. She tucks me into bed, folding a pink bunny into my arms and brushing the hair from my forehead.

"Looks like someone forgot your bed alarm." She leans

over and plugs something into the wall. "Good night. Please stay in bed, Dear."

"Yes mother." I say as she turns off the light. I squeeze the furry bundle in my arms and, with the blanket tucked tightly around me, start to feel warm again.

#

(February 1960)

I gaze at the swirls of plaster on our bedroom ceiling. The yellow glow in the room brings a flicker of excitement to this morning. To my right Carl is fast asleep. He still has a sweet boyish face that makes the dark hairs of his goatee look out of place. I slip from bed quietly, find my slippers and robe, and pad down the hall of our small home.

Scott is making soft noises in his bed as I pass his room. I quickly scoop the coffee into the percolator and plug it in. Scott's sounds become louder, I hurry back down the hall to his room where he's standing in his crib with a sour look on his face. His cloth diaper has soaked through causing a telltale wet circle on his pajamas.

Carl shuffles in as I finish getting the baby into a clean romper.

"How's the big man today!" he says as he leans over Scott and kisses his forehead.

"Dadadada." Scott reaches toward Carl and pokes his eye.

Carl kisses me on the cheek and goes to check on the coffee.

In the kitchen, I turn on the countertop radio and get out the Cheerios. I slide the bottle of milk and a bowl across the wooden table in front of Carl. He pours his cereal, lets out a deep sigh and begins to eat.

"You don't have much time, David will be here shortly," I prod looking at the clock.

He takes another bite of cereal, his slow morose chewing reminds me of a depressed cow.

Carl's not used to being up this early.

This past year, since we've been married, he usually sleeps in until noon then works on his sculptures or hangs out with his friends until late at night. He was supposed to be selling his artwork to support us, but he's only managed to sell two pieces in 12 months. Marylin sold her house and the fabric shop a few months ago. She gave us the money to get set up in this house as a "late wedding gift" before she moved down to Florida. I've been trying to be patient with Carl but bills are piling up and I'm done taking handouts.

Really, just his constant presence is starting to drive me insane.

I want to go to bridge with the other wives and mothers in the neighborhood in the afternoons. I want to do the normal housewife things but it's impossible with him criticizing everything about our life and boring the neighbors with his constant talk of civil rights and "the man."

But thankfully today is Carl's first day at the Fisher Body plant in Detroit. It's his first real job ever.

"Well, I suppose I better shave." Carl says with another deep sigh, plopping his spoon in his cereal bowl and rubbing his goatee. "They won't appreciate any Beatniks on the line."

I give him a sympathetic smile but I'll be glad to see it gone, none of the other wives husbands have facial hair.

I clear the table and make Scott his bottle. He fusses a little and turns to nuzzle my breast, the doctor recommended that he start bottle feeding to keep him strong but he's not used to it yet. He reluctantly turns back to the bottle, giving me a sulky look very much like his father's.

After Scott finishes his bottle, Carl re-enters the kitchen rubbing his smooth face as I run water to wash the dishes. "It's only temporary," he says to reassure me.

"Well, you still look handsome," I say and fake a pout. I pretend that I too will mourn the loss of our malaise and his goatee. He kisses me, and for the first time I feel the warmth and smoothness of his lips without the slight prick of his coarse facial hair.

"Thanks, Doll," he says with a wink.

The sound of my brother's honking car horn calls him outside.

Scott and I wave at him from the window. I finally feel like I can breathe with the space of the day before me.

#

With Carl at work, months pass and routine fills the house. The initial excitement over the idea of "free time" soon wanes. Baths, dishes, laundry, cooking, naps, repeat. I seem to always find new ways to fill the days with more tasks that amount to little. At night I am rocked to sleep by ticking off items from my to-do list.

As much as I finally feel like I'm getting the safe, normal life I've always wanted I can't help feeling let down. I wonder if I made the right choices, and I worry that I'll never be able to fit into the place I've carved out for us.

It seems Carl and I have so little in common anymore. I try not to regret being with him but he makes it hard, and that regret leads to fantasies about the road not taken. I often let myself wonder about how different things could be. Where was Paul now?

I enjoy my time alone with Scott. I push him in his stroller around the neighborhood in the afternoon, scenes from my own day playing out behind the windows and in the yards of our neighbors. It is reassuring to know I'm doing it right. I wave politely to Mrs. Holmes as we cross the street to head back to our house.

I lean down and kiss Scott's head. I inhale and take in his sweet baby smell. He takes the opportunity to grab a handful of my hair but I don't really want him to let go so I pick him up. We're just a couple houses from ours so I prop him on my hip and manage the stroller one handed.

When we get to our small house I sit on the step and squeeze his small frame close to me. He rubs his face into my shoulder leaving drool in my hair.

Old ladies in the grocery store are always pinching his cheeks and telling me to "cherish these moments," or "it goes so fast." I wonder if they are talking about his baby stage or the bond we have now. Either way it is mean advice, it always makes me panic a little because there is nothing I can do about the speed of time.

Cherished or not, the moments pass at the same pace. I pray my Scott and I will always be close. Even when he's grown and I'm old, I will stay near and see him and his family grow. Scott wraps his arms around my neck and pulls himself closer as if to reassure me that this is true.

#

(Present)

There's a light tapping on the door behind me, I don't look up. After a moment a man sits down next to me at the table. At first he looks old and I don't recognize him. Then I find an image in my mind and he looks young.

I've been sorting these buttons for what seems like hours. I couldn't find my mother's button box but I did manage to find some buttons from old clothes that we could use.

"If you want you can help me." I tell him after a moment. "We'll need to get this done before mom gets home. I can't do it by myself David." I give David a sharp look.

"Mom? Hey, how are you doing?"

I look up and study him, thinking about his words. I hear them but they don't make sense. It seems best not to reply.

David pulls his chair up and sits quietly, his face supporting a forced smile.

"Mom, look at me. It's Scott." He tries to hold one of my hands but I pull it away. I'm busy.

David's face falls and he starts to inspect one of the four large gold buttons grouped in front of him.

"Mom, where did you get these buttons?"

I give him a blank stare and a shrug, then snatch the button from his fingers.

"If you aren't going to help, then at least don't play with things, I'm always the one who does the work in this family."

"Mom, I'm not David. What happened to your shirt?"

David leans forward and points toward my chest where my cream colored bra is showing through my open shirt.

I look down and pull my shirt closed, all of the small white buttons are missing from the green blouse. I can't understand why he won't leave me alone, I'm busy.

David looks from my shirt to the table and back.

"Are all these buttons from your clothes? There must be dozens of buttons here." His face starts to flush as he scans the groupings.

"Nope, I think I was at, uh, 64 but I lost my place counting them." I shoot him a look.

He doesn't seem to hear me as he gets up and walks to the open closet. He rifles through a few items before he pulls out a wool jacket.

"Really? Even your coat?" He is looking from the heavy navy peacoat to the gold buttons on the table. He hangs the coat back up and opens the dresser drawers.

"Where are your clothes?" He asks loudly, slamming the drawer.

I look at him and laugh, "I put those in the laundry basket, they needed mending, you don't need to get excited."

He takes a deep breath and looks around the room. He spots a pile of clothes spilling out of a white basket and onto the floor.

"Oh, Jesus. Come on! Mom, this is your toilet!" He has his hands on his head and his lips pursed tightly together.

"I'll be right back mom." And disappears out the door.

I continue sorting the buttons on the table, inspecting each one carefully. When David comes back, Kay is in tow. He's speaking loudly, obviously agitated.

"Are you guys even watching her? Look at this?" He points to the commode laundry pile.

"And this!" The pitch of his voice raises, along with his eyebrows, as he sticks a finger in the pile of buttons.

He grabs one of the gold buttons, "These are from her coat, her winter coat, and it is snowing outside damn it!" he flings the button back on the table.

I rise slowly from my chair. "That's it! You aren't going to act like this! I have to take it from Dad but not from you, now go sit down while I'm trying to work!"

Kay's eyes are wide as she looks back and forth between mother and son, sister and brother. Scott rolls his eyes, takes a deep breath and looks at his feet.

"Alright, look sorry for getting loud. It's just, you're my mother, and I want to make sure you're taken care of."

I don't know what he's talking about. He's my son? Somewhere in the back of my mind, it seems it could be true. But David is not my son. I give up the thought, pull my shirt closed again and stare back at the two of them as they talk.

Kay clears her throat, "Scott, I'm sorry about this. She started taking a few buttons off of things last week but nothing like this. She was just out an hour ago when she took her meds...."

"Look, I know but we're going to have to figure something out. I'll have my sister come by and bring more clothes. I'll take these ones."

He takes the clothes from the commode and puts them in a linen laundry sack. He heaves the full bag over his shoulder, looks at me for a few seconds and kisses my head.

"Bye mom, I love you." I give no reply, he leaves the room with his heavy burden.

#

I slide the cold glass of dark pop back and forth on the wooden table, it leaves wet tracks behind and I smear them with my finger. The room is warm, there is a hum of comfortable conversation over the table covered with food and dishes. I smile to myself at the happy faces.

As I watch the group I start to feel like I should be doing something. I notice people filling their plates and eating. In front of me is a small empty plate. They must have started eating without me.

"So we just don't say grace before we eat anymore?" I ask loudly and bow my head in defiance at the crowded table.

"Mom!" Suzy hisses and pokes me in the thigh. "This is dessert and we already said the blessing before we carved the turkey."

She's leaning in close and I can see something green on her front tooth, I reach out to touch it.

"Stop! Come on, eat some pie." She swats my hand away, slides a slice of pie on my plate and shoves a fork in my hand. "Eat," she repeats forcefully.

I look at the fork and decide to comply. The first bite of the pie is mushy, it fills my mouth and makes me gag. I grab the glass of pop and chug it to wash the taste from my mouth. The bubbles make my eyes water and I gasp for breath as I finish the glass.

A small curly haired girl sitting across from me stares wide eyed, she can't be more than five.

"Do you like pop?" I ask her, she nods with a smile. I take another full glass of pop from the table and offer it to her. "You want a drink of mine?"

The little girl gets up on her knees and reaches across the table when a blonde sitting next to her snatches the glass from my hand.

"Doris! Lana cannot have Coke! The dye and sugars in this will have her hopped up for weeks!"

My empty hand is frozen over the table as I stare at the woman in surprise. The child, who doesn't look surprised, sits back in her seat with a groan.

"Mom come on, sit back." Suzy takes my arm and pushes me gently into my seat.

She looks at the blonde, "Laurie, that's my drink. Give it here. Thank God she didn't drink it, I think the rum would get her before the dye." Suzy gives a little laugh but the blonde doesn't even smile.

"Scott, maybe we should get Lana home. It's getting late." Laurie says, tapping a handsome older man's hand. He looks at me and smiles.

Smiling back I say, "My boy is named Scott too. He would be much younger than you though. He's off at college." My mind flashes images of Scott in his dorm room at State.

The blonde giggles now and gets up from the table.

"What's he studying?" The older Scott asks.

I think about his words but they start to dissolve and lose their meaning. I poke at the orange mush on my plate, unsure of what else to do, I take a bite of the pie.

I quickly grab my napkin, spit the bite into it, then furiously wipe my tongue with the napkin. "I don't like this," I gasp and push the plate away.

Scott looks a little alarmed. "Are you okay?"

"I'm tired, I think we better go home."

Suzy takes the plate of half eaten pie.

"Sure, no problem. Let me get your coat." She walks down the hall and disappears.

When I stand up the little girl comes to hug me. I try to kneel down to hold her but it feels awkward and she pushes free.

Scott, Suzy and the blonde, are huddled together in front of the coat closet. As I come closer, pieces of the conversation drift towards me.

"So what did he say he was doing today? Why couldn't he come?" Suzy has a hand on her hip.

"He's with *her* family, they have a cabin somewhere up north. He said he'd try to be here next year." Scott replies looking at his shoes, the blonde rubs his arm gently.

"Well, what about Christmas and all the other holidays between now and then? He quits on her and just quits on all of us?" Suzy's voice cracks and she crosses her arms in front of her. "This is insane, it's not like him."

"I think since Mom moved out he just doesn't know what to do. They've been together over 50 years, I don't think he knows how to be alone, you know?" Scott is still looking at his shoes.

"No, I don't know! This isn't how people act, especially when they love each other." Suzy's face is red with anger.

"He still loves her, but he's still here and she is...well.. gone." Scott replies quietly.

Suzy's hands start flying around and she says something I can't understand.

A tall grey haired man interrupts the group, "I think we need to get your mother home, honey. She's looking tired and this guy is turning into a pumpkin." He points two thumbs at himself then leans in and kisses Suzy.

"Did you see it's snowing Grandma Doris?" the young girl says excitedly as she runs and presses her face against the front picture window. I press my face against the cold window too. Gazing into the blackness with it's white highlights, I wonder who is gone.

#

(Present)

"Hey, Mom, you alright?"

I look over to see Scott's face peering quizzically at me through the partially closed door. I realize I have been standing near the closet staring at a photo of Scott as a baby, a heavy sadness lingers in my heart but I don't know why. "Oh, yes. Scott, hi. I'm fine, fine."

Scott's face lights up when I mention his name. He comes in and sits on the footstool near me. "That's right mom, I'm Scott. I love it when you remember me."

His joy releases some of the weight in my chest and I chuckle to myself. "Of course I remember you, you're my son. What sort of mother doesn't remember her son?"

I step over to my recliner and settle in.

Scott just smiles. "I wanted to tell you something important so I'm glad you're having a good day."

"Well sure, if you say the day is good then it must be so." I reach over to pat Scotts hand and he holds it in his. I feel how warm and soft his hands are. I look from his hands to his face and see his likeness to his father. After a moment, I realize he has been talking and is looking at me expectantly, I figure I have missed something.

"Mom, this is exciting news for us. It's a big opportunity." His eyebrows are raised, he is definitely waiting for something.

I smile a little and hope this is the right response. I pull my hand away to smooth a loose lock of hair from my face.

His eyes follow my hand and his smile drops. "Mom, don't be upset. I'll still come to see you, I'll bring Lana and Laurie. The visits will be better because they won't be little drop by visits, they can be longer because we'll have driven from Indianapolis just to see you!"

"Indianapolis? Who lives in Indianapolis? That's a long drive. I don't want anyone driving that far for me." I'm nervous inside and I feel like I'm losing someone. I stare at Scott, waiting for him to make me feel safe.

Scott looks disappointed. "Mom, *I* am moving to Indianapolis and it is not that far. But don't worry, it won't be for a few months." He looks like he wants to say more but is giving up.

My mind pulls up scenes of Indianapolis, from the only time I have been there.

"Indianapolis... you know I've been there. I took a bus to see Paul there. Have you been there?" The young man sighs in reply.

I still feel nervous so I focus on his tie, the pattern looks familiar. I'm searching the teardrop shapes and gold dots for a word.

"Mom, look at me."

"Paisley," I say and feel better.

When I look up at the man, his face is concerned. His dark eyes shadow while his brow furrows. The expression is very familiar. "Do you know who I am?" he says softly.

"Of course." I say trying to convince him, and me.

I know that I had it in my mind just a moment ago. I can still feel the whisper of it tingling but it's gone.

Deep, strong emotions swirl just below the surface. I look at his face and want to make him feel better. I reach out and pat his hand.

"I love you." I say, and know it is true.

He gives a half smile and his eyes brighten, he leans in to

kiss my cheek. "I hope you know I love you too Mom."

\#

6

(October 1961)

"I can't believe this, she was so young." My mother shakes her head at the newspaper.

I don't need to look up from rinsing the milk bottles to know what she's talking about. The news about Paul's mother's death has been the topic for days. Grace's obituary is at the top of the section in the Sunday paper.

"Services will be tomorrow afternoon, is Carl going with you?" My mother puts the paper down and stands next to me at the counter. She scans my face, while pretending to help with the bottles.

"I don't know mom, he works third shift now, sometimes doubles, he needs to sleep. I'll probably stay home with Scott."

I've debated this question with myself as well. Is it more appropriate for me to go to the services because I obviously knew the family or more socially inappropriate for the married ex-girlfriend to show up to comfort the family? I can't even say that I think Grace actually liked me.

"Doris! You've got to go. You were this close to being a part of that family" She holds her fingers only inches apart. "You don't want to look bitter. I'll go too, we can leave Scott with David. He'll be home just listening to music, or whatever he's been doing, since he quit the factory."

I know this funeral will turn into a social event and my mother needs an excuse to go for a first hand look. Paul's mother, disappeared from Indianapolis last week after leaving to get groceries. They found her car days later, flipped into a marshy watershed off of Interstate 465. The gossip is that she had taken pills and fell asleep at the wheel but the obituary just called it a tragic auto accident. Since her family is from Ypsi she'll be buried near her mother in the Highland Cemetery.

"Aren't you even curious about Paul? The paper said he's a decorated war hero, he was injured saving people from a collapsing tunnel!" My mother pleads as if seeing Paul is an incentive to go.

"I don't know, I haven't heard from him since I sent him his ring back."

My mother gives a grunt in response. I'm not sure that she, or anyone else in this town, believes that I broke it off with Paul. I do know she definitely thinks Carl was a step down.

After a pause she says, "Well, like I said, it would show everyone there were no hard feelings if you went instead of hiding out here."

She is at least right about the hiding part, I have avoided town as much as possible.

On Friday, I made the mistake of taking Scott to the grocery store and was hassled twice by women we had gone to school with.

Bonnie Redgrove baited me through lipstick spotted teeth

as she rang up my order. "You know Paul just left here a couple hours ago. He came in and bought some cigarettes. Have you seen him?"

She stared at my face with anticipation, clutching my bag of apples in her hand.

"Oooh, Doris, you should see him. He always was handsome, and he hasn't changed a bit."

She winked then licked her lips before they split into a wide grin. "So are you gonna go to the funeral?"

The half-smile and shrug I answered with was apparently not the reply she hoped for because she cocked her chin and huffed while she punched the keys on her register.

In the parking lot, I couldn't load my groceries fast enough to avoid Katie Perkins prattling on about how she saw Paul and his father at the Sidetrack Grill the other night and did I know he is a decorated war hero now?

I assured her I saw the newspaper article and that I was very happy for him but I really needed to get home.

I drove home from the store flustered and conflicted with comparisons of the past and the present.

The lense of time has been unkind to my heart, smoothing out any flaws Paul had and bringing back sweet memories of him. The way he looked in his football uniform, how he felt pressed against me while we danced at homecoming. What if seeing him now only proves to myself that I made a mistake, that I could have been happy with Paul?

And still my mother is insistent, "You can't ignore this Doris, the more you hide out the more you'll invite scandal. Bonnie Redgrove told her mother that you looked all heartbroken when she mentioned Paul at Von's Market Friday, she said you even asked if he had changed."

"What! Bonnie's been eating too much of that cheap lipstick to keep her damn stories straight! That is not how it went!"

I slouch down in my chair and hold my hands up in surrender.

"Alright, okay... It's just...I'm not sure," I stutter. "Let me talk to Carl and I'll call you about it tomorrow."

She rolls her eyes, and carries the milk bottles to the front door. "Fine, but really Doris, I'm sure Paul would appreciate your condolences."

Now I roll my eyes and get my mother's coat from the closet. I'm not sure I can take much more of this.

After my mother leaves, I sit on the front porch to enjoy the quiet. Carl and Scott have gone over to the hardware store to buy finish for a carving he's working on. I'm lost in thought, picking at the paint on our rocking chair when a small grey Ford truck pulls into the driveway.

I recognize the driver before he gets out but it takes me until he reaches the front step to register that Paul is at my house. I scramble to my feet and look around the neighborhood for peeping faces in windows.

"Paul, hey, oh my God I'm sorry about...." I trail off because he's staring so intently at me. I've forgotten how dark his eyelashes are and how the shade of his eyes change with his mood, right now they are a cloudy greyish green.

"I needed to see you." He blurts. "I waited so that no one was here. Can we talk?"

I'm unsure about what to do. No doubt someone will see us on the porch, if they haven't already. But being alone in the house with him seems worse, Carl could be home anytime.

"Carl will be home soon," Paul winces when I say this and I regret it. He takes a step backwards and I realize I want him to stay. "Just come and sit, we can talk out here."

Paul comes up the steps and leans against the railing. I sit back in my chair, taking in his height and broad shoulders. He seems to have grown up, he looks much more like a man now, not like the boy I last saw waving from the Indiana bus stop. We study each other until a breeze catches a few loose locks of my hair and dances them distractingly across my face.

"So, are you okay?"

His eyes close slowly, "No, I'm not. How can I ever be okay?"

I can't answer, I've asked the wrong question.

His lips press tightly together then his eyes lock onto mine, he speaks just above a whisper.

"Nothing is okay... my mom is gone... and you, you were my best friend you know? YOU are what I remember about this town. I can't be here and not see you."

His hand moves slowly toward me before he shoves it into his pocket and looks toward the unlit porchlight above the door. I can see the corners of his eyes glistening.

"My mom always thought we would get married."

He takes a few pacing steps along the rail, his face a mix of pain and agitation. "I know you thought she didn't like you, and maybe you weren't who she would have picked for me, but she always said nice things about you. She was genuinely sad when I told her about your letter." He stops and leans back again.

"That was the worst you know, getting that letter." He looks right at me, a guilty pang twists in my chest, it's my turn to look away.

"The ring fell out before I finished opening the envelope and I knew. I left the letter unopened for days. When I finally read it..." He clears his throat. "You know, there's no privacy in camp, there's no place to cry. I had to just take it with me, the pain and the loss and the anger, it went everywhere with me. I took it to Berlin, and that place is crazy. I had to keep it close since I knew I didn't have you." When I look back at Paul I see a tear on his cheek.

Two boys fly down the street on their bikes yelling at each other. Paul straightens up and wipes his face. My heart is breaking. I wish I had invited him in so I could at least hold him, and yet I'm so glad we're outside with propriety between us.

"Anyway, I just needed to see you. I heard you'd married Carl, ugh, I can't believe it was Carl. I had to see for myself, to see you as someone else's girl; to see you as someone's mother?" Although I know it isn't really a question, I feel like I have to answer.

"Yeah, yes, I am. I'm sorry. Well, not sorry but I am Carl's wife and Scott's mother." Saying it to him, I feel embarrassed, not proud like I usually do when I talk about Scott. I've been able to keep this me and the vision of who I was with Paul separate in my mind for the past two years, and now they've found each other out. I feel like I've been caught in a lie.

"I want you to come to my mother's funeral tomorrow." His eyes are soft and emotions raw. "Please, come." I could not hurt him again.

"Okay," I whisper and I feel like we've just broken up even though it's been years.

Paul walks down the front porch steps as Carl pulls up to the curb. Scott waves excitedly out the back window of the Chevy. Paul stops for a moment and stares at the car as Carl gets out. He walks around the car with his eyes on Paul. Paul gives a little wave and quickly gets into his truck. Carl continues to stare as the truck backs out to the street and pulls away. He carries Scott up the porch steps and gives me a questioning look.

"Was that Paul?" He lets Scott run ahead into the house.

"Yeah, he wanted to let me know his family hoped to see

me at the funeral." I clear my throat of emotion.

"Oh, his *family* wants you to go huh?" Carl's eyebrows are raised and his grin is cocked to the side of his face. He wants to tease me about this but I'm not sure I can play.

"Well, he said he knew I'd worry about it and that he's over everything and if I wanted to go then I was welcome." I start walking ahead of Carl so he can't see my face while I lie.

"Paul always was so thoughtful…" This time I don't need to see Carl's face to note his sarcasm.

"Ugh, come on Carl, don't stress me out over nothing." I turn, standing closer than necessary to him. "Play nice." I run a finger up his arm.

"Stop, don't distract me from antagonizing you." He says as he leans in for a kiss.

"Mommy!" Thankfully Scott interrupts and grabs my hand.

"Sorry Babe." I say with a forced grin and peck his cheek before I'm pulled off towards the living room.

#

Carl sleeps as I get up to get Scott ready for the day. Keeping quiet in our house during the day reminds me of being a teenager trying not to wake up my father when he passed out on the couch. Even though I want Carl to have this job, I can't help but feel some resentment as he lay asleep each day while I take care of everything.

"Shhh, baby boy. Let mama get you ready for a fun day with uncle David!"

My brother is watching Scott while my Mom and I go to the funeral. She offered to take Scott overnight in case I wanted to "get together" with any of the "old crowd." I guess she doesn't remember that Paul was really the only person in high school I hung out with. So there is almost no chance I'll be pulled into anyone's evening plans. Even so, I've really accepted her offer because I plan to enjoy some quiet time and a full night's sleep.

I stuff myself into the only black dress I own. It has long sleeves and a slim fit both by design and more so because I still have some extra baby weight. I made it when I still wanted to look older and fit in with Carl's friends. I wouldn't say it's appropriate for a funeral but it's the best I can do for now. Hopefully, I can borrow a shawl from my mother to cover some of my curves.

Our old house looks the same as when all four of us lived there, even though it's usually just the two of them. Even my father's work boots sit by the door, unworn for years. He disappears for longer and longer stretches now but no one talks about it.

"Alright, buddy, Mommy and Grandma have to go, can you stay and play with Uncle David?"

Scott looks from me to David and laughs. I hug him and give him a kiss before I put him down. He runs away into the living room yelling "ball! ball!"

"Good luck." I say to David as he chases after Scott.

We arrive at the visitation about a half hour in. The room is crowded and there's a long line to shake hands with the family. My mother steps in behind two older ladies, I try to sneak by her and veer toward the back of the room but she grabs my arm.

"You can wait with me and pay your respects."

I realize that I left the shawl she lent me back at the house, I suddenly feel exposed standing near the front of the room.

"I can go get us a seat." I attempt another escape but the look she gives keeps me in line.

When we get to the family I shake hands with Paul's

grandparents who don't recognize me. Next I shake hands with Gregg, Paul's father. He looks surprised to see me then pulls me in for a hug. I try to mutter some apologies but I'm not sure he's listening. "So glad you could come." He says, his voice shaking.

Paul is last in the line, my mother has to nudge me forward. I regret coming now and I briefly consider dashing for the door. Paul is still nodding to the person in front of me when I reach out to shake his hand, he doesn't realize it's me before we touch. Our eyes and hands meet at the same time. His hand is warm in contrast to my ice cold fingers. Electricity shoots through me, my eyes start to water. He holds my hand in both of his for a moment then steps in for a hug.

I'm awkward as I debate it's propriety even as it happens, I find my face buried in the pins and medals on his chest. I inhale deeply, he smells the same as he did in high school.

"Doris, thank you." He breathes in my ear, leaving me dizzy. My mind flashes to our last time together in the backseat of his car.

My mom nudges me again, bringing me back to the moment. I move along to find a seat in the back of the room. I'm surprised to find that my face is already wet with tears.

#

(Present)

I don't know how long I've watched the robins at the feeder, but my rumbling stomach reminds me that the birds are not the only ones who need to eat. I wander down the hall to the kitchen and find the refrigerator. I give the handle a tug but it doesn't open.

Another firm tug causes the porcelain chicken sitting on the top of the fridge to rattle in her nest.

"Damn it!" I say as I give a whole hearted jerk. This time the chicken is completely unsettled and shatters on the floor.

"Oh, no! Oh no!" I take a few steps back and steady myself at the sink.

A little man with an accent comes running around the corner. "Mrs. Doris, are you alright! What happened!"

The roundness of the surprise at his eyes and mouth are comical to me, and I can't help but laugh.

"No Mrs. It's not funny. Are you hurt?" He hops over the field of porcelain shards and begins to inspect me.

"My goodness, I'm not hurt. But that thing there," I point at the pieces, I can see the word in my head but it won't come out. "That thingy, is not going to make it."

He holds my arm to guide me around the mess, over to the table where I sit.

"I'm hungry and that door won't open." I wave my hand toward the refrigerator. "Must be jammed, should we call some-one?"

"No, it's locked, not jammed, Mrs. Doris. Let me clean this up then I'll get you something." He grabs a broom and starts sweeping.

I'm thinking about this word "locked," I toss it around in my brain to look for its meaning. "Locked, locked, locked" I say to myself.

A few pictures flash through my mind of doors shutting, the little knobs on their handles being turned with a click. I look around the room from my seat and find nothing familiar. Next a black and white image of a barred door sliding shut replays in my mind and I come to a reasonable conclusion. "I'm locked here."

"What Mrs. Doris?" The man asks and leans on his broom.

"I'm locked here. You won't let me go home. I'm locked here."

"Mrs. did you say you were hungry? Can I get you an apple?" He steps closer to me, cocking his head sideways, ignoring my comment.

"Why can't I go home? I just want to go home." I repeat and stand up, taking a few steps towards the door.

The man looks at me like he's trying to decide something. The pause makes me more uneasy.

"Now Doris," he speaks very slowly. "Let me get you a snack, then we can talk about going home. Would you like an apple or some Lorna Doones?" He moves quickly and takes the items from the bowl on the counter.

"Or would you like both? You can choose Mrs. Doris. Choose." He waves them both in front of me.

The shiny yellow package of the cookies is distracting. Why won't he hold them still? I remember those cookies. Something is tugs at my mind. I feel like a question is unanswered. I've lost it in the midst of this man's accent, his movements and his questions. I'm anxious but can't remember why. I stare at the cookies as they bob up and down in the man's hand. My stomach growls audibly.

"You're hungry, take the apple Doris. It's good for you."

I take the apple and sit back in my chair. Something is still unresolved but I let it go and watch the man sweep white shiny fragments from the floor.

#

"Mom?"

I open my eyes to see Suzy peek through the doorway. I've dozed off in my chair, waking to her face is comforting.

"Oh, Suzy." I smile and reach my hand out to her. I see it tremble slightly. It surprises me with its shaky, spotted oldness.

When I say her name, relief washes over her face and she smiles back. "Looks like you're doing well today."

"I suppose I am. Aren't we lucky?" I chuckle to myself. I lean over and pat the footstool near me.

"Now tell me all about your new husband, what's his name?" I twirl my finger in the air trying to conjure it up.

"His name is Steven and he isn't new mom, we've been married for 8 years." Suzy rolls her eyes and digs in her purse.

"Eight years, well then where are my grandkids?"

She pulls her phone out and kneels down next to me. A photo of Suzy and a handsome grey haired man pop up. She swipes her finger on the screen and another photo shows a young couple on the beach with a toddler.

"Well, this is your granddaughter Melissa and her husband Chris. And this is your great grandson Sawyer."

"Huh, he's a cutie." I'm a little confused by the ages of the people in the photos and Suzy's husband doesn't look familiar.

"I thought your husband looked different."

"Well, I was married before Steven to Jim. Maybe you are thinking of him?" she shrugs.

I look at her phone again. "Maybe, do you have a picture of him in there?"

Suzy laughs, "No! Mom, who carries around pictures of their ex-husbands? Steven would have a fit!"

I smile and shrug. I reach out and stroke Suzy's hair.

"You know I'm so lucky to have you. You are my special

girl."

Suzy smiles slightly and holds my hand, her large green eyes crinkle at the corners. "Thank you mom, it's nice to hear."

"You remind me of your father. I've always loved that about you."

Suzy's smile fades, she squeezes my hand and looks away.

"Thanks Mom, I've always thought I looked more like grandma though."

I look at her shiny red hair. "Well, maybe…" I try to picture my mother in my mind.

"See look." Suzy unhooks a picture from it's nail on the wall and brings it closer. It's a faded picture of my mother, holding a toddler in front of our house.

I look from Suzy to the picture and back. "Well, the hair is the same, but the eyes are definitely your fathers."

She looks a little disappointed but smiles at the picture before she hangs it back up.

"Let's talk about something else." She looks around the room, the birdfeeder in the window catches her eye. "Have you seen any robins lately?"

I think hard. "I don't think so."

#

7

(October 1961)

After the funeral we head over to the VFW, it's just a few blocks from my mother's house. She chatters on about her friends at, gossiping about their children. I nod and smile at her comments, I'm trying to keep my courage and my stomach. I'm still shaken by seeing Paul, how touching him, hit me so hard.

"So, just don't tell anyone I told you she wears a wig, okay?" My mother finishes as we park her car on the street.

"Uh, sure mom." I mutter and we head into the hall.

I'm poking at my potato salad when Paul sits down next to me. We are in the farthest corner from the food and my mother has wandered off with a couple gossipy ladies from church.

"Are you hiding?" he asks as he scoots in his chair.

"I'm not sure." I say and focus on the salad.

"You know, I've never seen you drink." He pushes a glass in front of me. "Have a drink with me Doris."

The way he says it sounds like a dare.

I pick up the drink and try to read his face. His demeanor makes me nervous, there is something mixed with the sadness I don't recognize.

I take a long swig and put the half empty glass on the table.

"I usually don't drink and we were just kids. Where would we have drank? On the roof?"

He smiles, his voice is smooth and wistful, "Ahh, the roof. Some of my fondest memories."

Paul and I share another drink and, for a bit it's like old times, like life is still ahead of us.

"Remember when we broke the window? My mom's face was priceless. That was crazy." He chuckles to himself. "We were crazy."

I laugh at this. "WE were never crazy. We always played by the rules. We probably should've spent more time being crazy."

He looks away, the room is starting to clear and the church ladies are cleaning up. A few quiet seconds pass before he speaks again.

"Well, I'm more than willing to be crazy now Doris. Life is too short."

He looks at me like he has a decision to make, then puts his hand over mine on the table. "Come with me, let me take you somewhere."

I move my hand before anyone sees. "Paul…" But he interrupts. "Really Doris, don't overthink it. Let's be crazy, just once together, for old times sake."

I search his face for a hint of his intentions but find only a mischievous grin. His green eyes are clear and bright, he reminds me of his younger self. A warmth flushes my face, either from the drink or the memories.

"Come with me. I do have something to show you."

Even though I know I shouldn't, I nod my head.

"Meet me out that side door in a minute. I have a plan." He disappears and, after I slam the rest of my drink, I sneak out the side door. I stand casually along the exit drive keeping a lookout until Paul pulls around with the truck. He leans over and pushes the door open, I jump in.

"Duck," Paul says as we drive toward the front of the building. I slide down in the seat as we pass a group gathered on the lawn of the VFW.

"I think we're safe," Paul says. I slide back up in the seat. I'm torn between panic and excitement.

"No, we are not safe! This is insane, anyone could see me in your truck and there would be no end to the tongue wagging around here." Exasperated, I cover my face. "What are we doing."

Paul laughs, "Look, it's getting dark anyway and no one really knows this truck. Calm down. We're just two old friends reminiscing, we haven't done anything wrong."

Paul pulls a bottle of Blackberry brandy from under the seat. "Here, relax." He hands me the bottle.

I take a long slug and make a face. It's warm and too sweet but I take another slug before I hand it back. Paul laughs.

"It's not what I would pick to drink. Wine maybe, but not brandy from a bottle." I say defensively.

"Yeah, me neither but it's what I could reach when I snagged it from behind the bar before I left."

"Oooh, stealing liquor, you have turned into quite the rebel." I chastise him with a grin.

After a few blocks we are parked in front of Paul's old house. It looks exactly the same as it did when he lived there. The house is completely dark.

"It doesn't look like anyone is home." Paul raises his eyebrows with a thought, "Should we see if we can still get up on the back porch roof?"

"What, no! Paul are you nuts!" I slap at him playfully. "Let's get out of here before anyone sees us."

Paul pulls away from the house and soon we are on the freeway.

"Now where are we going?" I giggle and take a swig of brandy. Paul doesn't answer but reaches over and smooths my hair I turn my head into the warmth of his hand.

We pull into the Highway Motel parking lot.

"This is where I'm staying." He announces as if it explains what we're doing here.

Grabbing the brandy, he hops out of the truck and comes around to open the door for me.

"You can't bring me here." I cross my arms clumsily, I'm aware of the oncoming effects of the alcohol.

"I really do have something to show you," he says with a smile.

I hesitate, debate his motives again, then take his hand and slide out of the truck. The motel has outside entrances, so within a few quick steps we are in his room.

The room is tidy with things stacked precisely on the dresser, his suitcase is open on the stand with more items neatly arranged inside.

"I didn't unpack or anything. I wasn't sure how long I would stay." He says, following my gaze.

Handing me the brandy bottle, he points to the one chair in the room. "Why don't you sit, it will just be a minute."

He takes off his dress uniform jacket and hangs it on a

hook. He unbuttons a few buttons on his shirt then starts to dig in a black leather bag next to the sink. I try to keep looking around the room but I'm drawn to watching him. His shoulders are much broader than I remember, I can see the muscles moving under the thin shirt. A narrow line of sweat has marked the place between his shoulder blades.

"Here we are." He gives me a boyish grin.

In his hand he holds a small velvet bag. It dangles from his fingertips by delicate gold strings. "I bought this for you, but I never got to give it to you."

His face is soft but serious.

He sits on the corner of the bed, his knee touching the inside of mine. I can feel his warmth.

"Open it." He whispers.

"I don't think I should."

"You have to open it. You have to see what I wanted to give you." He turns my hand and gently lays the soft bag in my palm.

"It won't do any good Paul. I don't want to see it."

He takes the bag out of my hand and turns it over. A smooth gold band with a small square diamond falls into my palm.

"There are some things you can't return, things you can't take back." He closes my fingers around the ring.

"I love you Doris, and when I saw you again I knew. I just can't take it back."

My heart leaps with fear and relief. My head is swimming.

The old feelings for Paul remind me that things were unfinished. I thought that if I just buried them deep they would fade, but as I look at Paul now I know they haven't faded.

But they need to stay buried.

"Paul, no, I'm sorry..." He slides quickly onto his knees and pushes his lips to mine before I can finish.

I should keep protesting but the old yearning is convincing.

There's only a moment between right and wrong, with a breath I choose to give in and forget. I can't think and I don't want to. I drop the ring and run my hands through his hair. He holds my face and kisses me gently.

I can feel him tremble as our bodies press together. He picks me up and holds me so tight I can barely breathe. "I just want to squeeze you until you're a part of me."

His mouth is hot on my neck and my hands search for access to his skin. I want to melt into into him as we lower onto the bed, I can't remember the last time I felt this heat.

For the next few hours we are tangled together under the sheets, between giggles and dreams. There are murmurs of the love we shared and I feel young. He tells me stories of his service in Berlin. We talk about his family, and my parents. We don't mention Carl or Scott. During this time, they are suspended from our reality. During this time we might have a future.

Soon Paul drifts to sleep. He presses my hands to his lips and says "stay, always stay." I lay awake wondering what to do now. My heart is full and aching. I slip out of bed, gather my things and slink to the bathroom.

Paul is snoring when I emerge, still disheveled but dressed. I find my shoes and spot Paul's keys on the table. I can leave his truck at the VFW and get my car from my mom's.

If I wake him it'll be worse. The idea of riding back with him, having to ruin the tiny bit of magic we created by smearing it with drama and excuses is too much. The result will be the same. We can't see each other again.

I write a quick note on motel stationary and tuck the keys

in my purse. I tip toe to the door, shoes in hand, and almost yelp when I step on something sharp. I reach down and pick up the diamond ring.

I hold it for a minute, watching it sparkle in the thin light through the window. I slip it on next to my wedding band before I disappear.

#

Present

Suzy and Scott sit closely together at the kitchen table. Scott turns the ring on his finger nervously. There are piles of papers arranged neatly in front of them. Kay hands me a mug of coffee then gets them each a glass of water. She clears her throat before she begins.

"Obviously, you see she's getting worse. Which we expected, but we need to consider what to do when we can't manage her in this home anymore."

Kay pauses, looking sympathetic and tired. "She is up at night more, it makes it hard for other residents - as well as staff."

"Are you saying she has to go?" Scott asks with alarm.

"No, not yet, but this is a group home. It's not really set up for people with late stages of Alzheimer's. We love Doris, and your family, but if we keep having this many incidences," she points to the stack of yellow papers, "then she will have to find a better suited facility, it's not safe."

"We're going to need your help Kay," Suzy gives her a knowing look .

I watch the conversation more than listen. My head turns from speaker to speaker but the words stay at a distance, unregistered. No one looks at me so I assume I'm not expected to say anything.

Kay shrugs. "Honestly, whenever you find a place I would move her. If you don't already have a place in mind it could take a while. Good places are hard to come by...."

"This is going too fast. She's only been here, what, a year?" Scott stands and paces. "Are you giving her the meds? Aren't they supposed to slow it down?"

Suzy groans, "Scott, come on, it's been two years and who knows if the meds are doing anything anyway. It is what it is, now calm down." She nudges the chair next to her and he returns to his seat. "You're acting like Dad."

"Right now, I'm going to take that as a compliment." He says with a sigh.

"Do you have any ideas of places that are good?" Suzy gets her phone from her purse and taps at the screen.

"Honey, I would keep her out of the nursing home downtown. It looks pretty but I never hear anything good about that place."

"You think she needs a nursing home?" Now Suzy looks alarmed.

"Well no, but there's only one memory care facility in Ypsilanti and I doubt it has an opening. It costs a pretty penny." Kay rubs her thumb across her fingers pointedly.

Suzy leans back in her seat and gives Scott a slap on the shoulder. "I guess we're going to have our work cut out for us brother."

Scott sighs, "I suppose so, but I don't know how much help I'll be. This isn't really what I'm good at. We're getting ready to move in the next few weeks. I just don't have time." He spins his ring again and looks at the floor.

Suzy smirks. "Of course not." The two siblings lock eyes

and the tension in the room raises.

Kay stands abruptly, bumping the table. I watch water slosh over the edge of one of the glasses.

"These are your copies," she says pushing a file at the pair. "I need to get the lunch meds ready now. Let me know when you have a plan."

For the first time they both look at me, I shrug and look out the window where I see a pot bellied woman being pulled along the sidewalk by a fluffy white dog.

Taking a long sip of my coffee, I have the feeling something is about to change.

#

(October 1961)

I park Paul's truck at the VFW. It's dark and the streets are quiet. Now that I'm here I'm not sure this was the best plan. I toss the keys under the floor mat and walk away from the truck as quickly as possible. I take the long way around the building to avoid being seen from the street.

I step onto the sidewalk and hear a dog yip behind me.

"Oh, hello there."

A high pitched voice scolds the dog as the shadow stoops and picks it up. "Now be quiet Coco. Don't worry, she's not a biter. Just makes a lot of noise. Is that Doris McArther?"

I smile at the old woman as she steps closer to me. "It's Atkins now, Mrs. Starkweather. But yes it's Doris."

"Oh, yes, of course." She looks me over. "It's a nice night for a walk?"

I straighten my dress and clutch my purse to my chest.

"Um, yes, I was just getting some air after the long day. I'm going back to my mother's now." I say and make a wide arc around her. "You have a great evening."

Mrs. Starkweather's voice follows me as I cross the street. She mutters a drawn out goodbye. I walk as fast as I can without running to cover the two blocks to my mother's house. I let out a sigh of relief when I finally get to the car. There's a light on in the house, the dashboard clock says it is 9:45, I know Scott will be asleep by now. I just hope my mother doesn't notice me leave.

On the drive home I replay the day in slow motion. The funeral, Paul, the hotel, the ring.

What have I done? Why would I do that? Did I just ruin my whole marriage? I don't think I can breathe.

I pull over to get myself together. The diamond ring, still nestled close to my wedding band, catches my eye. Carl never gave me a diamond, just that first clay ring then this gold band. The diamond looks so new next to the band tarnished by washing dishes and folding laundry.

Did I toss away the life I want for my children? I *had* fantasized about Paul over the past year and I love that he still wants me. Do I still love him? I can't honestly tell myself I didn't know what I was doing, that I didn't know what was going to happen. Of course I knew, but why would I do that?

I think about Paul's smile, his touch, I quiver. It felt like a time when I still believed I could leave this place; when I felt I was the center of someone's world. Today, for a few hours, there were more possibilities.

Only now, all the frightening, reality changing possibilities loom in front of me. I feel like Dorothy watching the Wizard float away in the balloon. I realize there is no place like home, and I am a fool.

With my forehead on the steering wheel I weep, a desperate mournful cry. I let it out until there is nothing left.

Carl can never know and I'll never tell him. Paul certainly won't want to start drama after his mother's funeral. I'll hide out at home for the next few days.

Oh, God, I hope Paul leaves soon, he has no reason to stay. I catch my breath, start the car and drive home.

No one will ever have to know.

But for me there is no way to forget.

#

(Present)

I won't leave my room.

The people who hold me here try to lure me out with food and promises of "fun" games. The woman insists that this is my home but when I peek out the door, nothing is familiar. At least in this room there are a few items I recognize. My senior portrait, the afghan I made when Scott was born and a photo of Suzy with Scott at the beach.

I'm not sure about the other items. Some of them feel familiar but I can't place them. I pick up a white Bible from the nightstand and look at the inside cover, I see my maiden name scrawled under the picture of an angel. I toss it on the bed and pick up the wooden box the Bible was resting on.

I open it and "Somewhere Over the Rainbow" plays in tin melody slowly then stops. The box is lined in red satin. A few ear-rings, a rose brooch, and bits of old paper are scattered between the sections. I pull a gold satin ribbon and the upper level, lifts out. Inside this deeper, secret compartment are two black velvet boxes.

I pluck one of the boxes from its hiding place and flip open the lid. Inside rests a tarnished gold band in a pillow of black satin. It feels weighted, solid when I hold it.

I try to put it on my bare left ring finger but my swollen knuckles won't let it move more than a third of the way. Frustrated, I push until it digs into my skin and I have to give up. I twist off the ring and press it to my lips before I tuck it safely back into its home.

I slide the box back into the compartment and pick up the other. Just then the door swings wide and a tired looking woman barges in with a tray.

"Doris, you've got to eat a bit today so you can take your meds." She looks around for a place to set the tray and clunks it down on the open night stand. I shove the black box under my pillow.

"I brought some coffee, some soup and a sandwich. I think it's turkey, I can't remember." She's talks without looking at me and digs in her pocket. She pulls out a small plastic container and shakes it at me.

"These are your meds. It's almost noon and you haven't taken any yet. That's not a good thing, okay Doris?"

She grabs the wooden jewelry box from my lap and deposits it near the footboard.

"Just in case you need a sip to move things along," she pushes a styrofoam cup into my hand.

She takes a spoon and cup of applesauce from under a napkin.

"So I'll help you get started with a few bites of applesauce and get these meds taken care of." She trails off, starting to hum as she dumps a couple of pills onto the heaping spoonful of applesauce.

She leans in and makes an "ahh" sound coming toward me with the spoon. I pull my lips together and lean back on the bed.

The woman takes a breath and stands back up. "Seriously Doris, this is something you HAVE to do. Your doctor ordered these and your kids want you to take your meds."

I narrow my eyes and take a sip of water. I find I'm very thirsty and finish the cup. The smell of the soup makes my stomach growl audibly. "Look Doris, even your stomach wants you to take these pills. Let's get it over with."

I try to decide why these meds are important. I can't remember being sick or the last time I was at a doctor.

It seems like I've been locked up here a while. I consider asking why I need them but the spoon is still hovering so near my mouth that I'm afraid if I open it to talk she'll shove it in before I can speak.

"Gavin!" yells the woman to the open door, seconds later a short man appears. "Yes, ma'am," he says with an accent.

"Please call Suzy and ask her to speak with her mother about her meds," The woman is still poised with the spoon so I remain still.

The man pulls a phone from his pocket and pushes a few buttons. Soon a ringing fills the room and then I hear Suzy's voice answer. "Hello?" she does not sound happy. I can't resist and start speaking, "Suzy? Suzy! It's me."

Gavin interrupts and announces loudly, "Mrs. Doris is not behaving and will not take her medicine today. Ma'am, can you tell her it's okay."

I hear a sigh and a groan, "Mom. Yes, please take your medicine. You know they'll help your memory and your heart pill keeps you from having a stroke, so please take them. Okay?" She speaks fast. I'm trying to come up with the words for a response.

"Mom, say, 'yes I will take my medicine'." I hear the impatience in her voice and can read it on the faces of my warden's.

I start to open my mouth when she interrupts, "Mom listen, I need you to say, I-will-take-my-medicine. Say it now so I can hear you."

I think about the words and my mouth begins, "I…." I trail off and Suzy tries again, this time breaking it down into two words segments so I can repeat each one.

I repeat the words obediently, as soon as the word medicine leaves my lips the spoon is again thrust toward me but this time I don't resist. I open up and swallow everything they give me.

"Good, good, Doris. Thanks so much Suzy. She's being difficult today." The woman shouts at the phone.

"Yeah, alright Kay. I need to get back to work now. Oh, love you mom." And she hangs up before I can reply.

My mouth is sticky with applesauce, I take a long drink of water from the cup still in my hand. "I love you." I hear myself mutter.

"Do you need help with your lunch Doris?" Kay asks as she uncovers the food on the tray, "your soup is probably almost cold by now."

I shake my head and continue to hold the straw in my mouth even though I'm not drinking. "Okay then, I'll be back to check on you in a bit." She and Gavin bustle back through the door leaving it open behind them. I get up and shut it. I sit back on the edge of the bed and stare at the soup. I'm not hungry so I lay back on the bed to rest.

When my head hits the pillow I notice there's a lump underneath. I reach under it and pull out a small black velvet box. Inside, a small square diamond ring sparkles like magic. I press it to my lips before sliding it back in the box under my pillow and drift to sleep.

#

8

"Hurry up Doris or we'll be late!" Carl calls through the bathroom door.

When I finally appear in the hallway, he's in the kitchen pulling our plastic wrapped dish-to-pass from the refrigerator.

He already has Scott in the car and has come back in twice to get me.

"I'm so fat! This isn't right, I shouldn't go out like this." I'm whining and I don't even care.

"My God Doris you're pregnant, you're *supposed* to be fat, come on!"

I shoot him a look and stomp to the door, "Fine. Look at me! I'm wearing a tent." I do a spin in my dress with its pleated jacket that hides the 7 months of my baby's existence.

He takes my hand and kisses it. "Hey, I'm sorry. You're beautiful. You'd outshine a Kennedy, even a pregnant Jackie, now please let me take you to the reception and show you off."

My cousin's wedding was held at the church an hour ago and we're just now leaving for the reception because I was afraid Scott wouldn't sit still in the hot crowded pews.

From the door, I can see Scott jumping around in the back seat. I roll my eyes and start out to the car with the gift.

When we arrive, everyone is lining up to eat. I quickly slide my Jell-O salad onto the end of the buffet and scan the room for the gift table.

I spy it across the room and try to creep unnoticed along the edge of the crowd but bump belly first into the sturdy back of a familiar form.

The wide shouldered man turns and I stare up into Paul's boyish face.

I'm speechless.

Actually, we're both speechless. He stares at the bulge of my stomach peeking from my jacket.

"Paul come on, I'm starving!" a tall brunette tugs Paul by his sleeve and they dissolve into the crowd.

I try to sink into the wall because I cannot command my legs to move. My mind is flooded with images of Paul.

The last time I saw him was months ago. He was begging me to stay with him as we lay together in his hotel room after his mother's funeral.

It had never occurred to me that he could be here.

My thoughts are interrupted by my mother.

"Doris, are you okay? Let me take that for you, why don't you go sit with Carl." She takes the small white box from me and points over to the table where Carl and Scott are sitting.

"Mommy, mommy, see!" Scott points at the paper bell that serves as the centerpiece of our table.

I try to wake from my shock, my voice cracks as I reply, "Oh so pretty, yes baby."

Carl looks at me with concern, "Babe, are you feeling sick?"

"Yes," I answer honestly and take a seat.

"Okay, picture time!" My aunt holds her camera and waves Carl and I closer together. Scott has disappeared under the table somewhere.

I notice Paul sitting a few tables away, our eyes meet.

"Say cheese!" The flash of the camera is startling.

"I really don't feel well, maybe we shouldn't stay."

"Sure doll, let me say hello and goodbye to a few people, then we'll get out of here. Are you going to be alright?"

"Yeah, I just need some air, I'll meet you outside." I make sure my mother has Scott and escape through the side door.

I walk as fast as possible to the back of the building where we parked. As soon as I get near the car I rip off the heavy pleated jacket. Between the heat, the pregnancy and Paul I feel like I am suffocating.

Sitting on the large back bumper of a Chevy, I put my head in my hands and try to hold back tears. The back door of the Legion slams loudly, I look up and see Paul coming towards me.

I get up and walk towards a huge memorial statue of two soldiers carrying an injured comrade.

"Doris, stop!" I hear Paul quicken his steps, he catches me just on the other side of the statue. We both look around to make sure we're alone.

"What! Why are you even here?" I ask curtly.

"You just left. You snuck out on me. Don't you owe me an explanation?"

"No, the explanation should be obvious Paul."

He stares down at my stomach "How pregnant are you?... is that my baby?"

"No, and don't worry about it." I try to move around him.

He steps in front of me and leans down slightly. "How far along are you, how do you know that isn't our baby?"

"Jesus Christ Paul!" I say peeking around again. "No matter what, it is not *our* baby. I am married to Carl. I have a family. You know this."

"But you don't love him. I know *that*. We are meant to be together. You know it too, we are *meant* to be. Look at me…. Doris… Please."

The tears have returned, I stare at my feet."No, I don't know that."

"You left, you moved on. So did I. It doesn't sound like it was meant for anything but memories. And last time, well, we made a mistake." I clear the lump from my throat. "We've made so many mistakes."

"But I love you. I have *never* moved on. Just look at me, Doris." He whispers.

I smell whiskey on his breath and I suddenly feel the urge to vomit.

"No." I say, walking quickly back toward the car.

"Doris!" I hear him close in behind me, he grabs my elbow swinging me around. The movement is too much, leaning over, I start to purge.

The door of the hall slams again and there is Carl's voice.

"What the hell? Doris are you okay? Man, what are you doing?" There's the sound of hurried steps in the gravel.

Paul backs up, I feel Carl run his hand over my back. "Are you okay?" he whispers sweetly, I nod. My legs go weak and I kneel completely to the ground.

"Go on Paul, leave my *wife* alone. She doesn't need anyone watching her be sick." Carl stands squarely between Paul and I. "I'll take care of her."

I see Carl's hands worked into fists. Paul's face is red and he steps closer to Carl so they are only inches from each other.

"You make sure you do." He says and gives me a hurt look before he strides back into the building.

Carl watches him go then turns to me. "Really, are you okay?" he asks again.

I stand and lean against a nearby car. He hands me his handkerchief. "What the hell was that about?"

I can't answer, my throat is tight and I have no words. He apparently doesn't expect a reply. He pulls me in close, I feel safe for the moment.

#

(Present)

I only see darkness, I'm not sure that my eyes are really open. I feel heavy and horribly sad. My face is wet from tears, my nose is full and swollen. My arms are around my knees, the carpet is rough under my curled toes. The wall behind me and on my side lets me know I'm in a corner.

I slide my hands on the floor and find a shoe, then heavy smooth pieces of paper. I crawl, moving along the wall and away from the corner.

Within inches I bump my head on another wall. Reaching up I feel smooth wood. Under the weight of my hand the wall moves and I realize it's a folding door, a closet door?

Pushing harder, the door slides and late evening light illuminates a few familiar objects in the newly revealed room.

I crawl just outside the closet and sit up against the wall. Looking around, it takes a moment to get my bearings.

There's something stuck to the bare skin of my leg. I peel a piece of thick paper from my shin and find it's a picture.

A color photo of a beautiful family in a portrait studio. Father, mother, son and daughter, all dressed in red sweaters.

I begin to cry again because I know this is me and my family and I miss them. I can't remember where they are now but I know they are gone. I know I can't get them back.

The room suddenly lights up, Kay stands in the doorway.

"Oh my Jesus, are you hurt?" She looks alarmed.

I shake my head but tears continue to fall. Her eyes scan the mess around me. Comming closer, she gingerly lowers herself to the floor, groaning with the effort, until she's situated across from me. She pulls tissues from her fanny pack and stuffs them in my hand.

Kay picks up a photo and smiles at it. "Doris, it looks like you've had a lot of good times in your life."

She hands me the picture. It's of Carl, Scott and I sitting in front of a table with lots of decorations around us.

Carl has one arm around my back and one hand rests on my obviously pregnant belly. He looks into the camera smiling. Scott peeks from beneath Carl's chair and I'm looking away somewhere to my left. My hand hovers near my chin and it looks like I'm stifling a smile.

Only when I look at the photo I don't feel like I'm really smiling.

She points to Carl "Do you know who that is?"

"Carl," I whisper.

"And who is this?" She asks, pointing to the peeking toddler.

"My Scott," I say with a smile, looking at his chubby face.

"And who is in here?" She asks grinning because our game

is going so well.

I want to say Suzy, but the name can't find its way from my brain to my mouth. In a moment it's lost. I just feel sadness. My stomach turns, I don't like this photo.

"Stop asking all these questions, I don't like baby games." I push away the photo.

Looking around I see papers, photos, shoes and purses spilling from the closet. I pick up another photo of a young man with a goatee smiling in front of a van full of other young people.

I push the photo into Kay's hand. "My stuff is everywhere, this closet is a mess. Someone better clean it up before everything is ruined."

Kay struggles to rise from the floor. "Let's get you up now."

She steadies herself then reaches her arms under my shoulders. I place my hands on her biceps. She squats and pulls up, I'm barely able to haul myself to a half kneel, then I have to lean against the wall. We both breath heavily.

"OK, one more try old girl," she says and puts her arms under my armpits again, this time we're almost close enough to hug.

She squats and pulls. I push with my arms against the wall until I find myself standing. We take a moment to catch our breath, but I'm impatient to sit down again.

"What were you doing down there anyhow?" She asks leaning her thick arm against the door frame.

"Hell if I know." I say pushing by her on my way to the recliner.

#

(August 1963)

I'm face down with my head buried in the pillows of our bed. Suzy yells from her crib and the theme song from the Beverly Hillbillies blares from the TV room.

I just need a minute before I can go out there. I groan into the mattress and count to ten.

I roll out of bed and check the mirror. It's worse than I thought.

I look exactly how I feel; tired, overwhelmed, and sour. The red tint of my hair looks rusty and the makeup I applied yesterday has melted into the creases under my eyes. My face is shiny and my shirt sticks to me with the August heat.

I walk out to get Suzy but she's settled herself trying to shove a stuffed pink bunny through the rails of her crib. I peek in on Scott, he's happily sorting marbles and watching TV.

Carl comes in from outside, our eyes meet, I can tell he has been crying. Neither of us has slept much the last few days. He nods at me and I follow him to the back porch.

"I'm leaving tonight."

"Fine," I knew he would go. "I just wish you would stay."

He looks at me; his eyes are pleading and hurt.

I try to undo it.

"I know things will be different with us, I'm so sorry. If you go, I don't know how we'll survive on our own." I've already said this a dozen times, I can't change anything.

"Doris, you lied to me. LIED about our family, LIED to keep me here. It's not going to work anymore. You don't love me - you need me, and I *love* you, oh, God, I love you so much," his voice is strained, I can hear the tears coming.

"But I don't *need* you." His voice is a whisper.

"What about the kids, they love you, Scott adores you, this isn't their fault." I'm pleading; I know I'm playing a dangerous game.

Carl slides down on the step; he looks up at me with his large dark eyes and his unshaven face.

"How can you do this to someone? Look at me, I'm in shreds before you and still you want more."

There is silence.

I'm not proud of myself but I don't know how to get a hold of the situation. I feel it slipping through my fingers.

Carl breaks the silence. "She isn't mine."

"You don't know that..."

"And neither do you, dammit. God dammit Doris!" He stomps his foot like a child. I reach out but he moves into the yard, far from my touch.

"I just need some time," He is serious, resolved. "I'm going with the group to the capitol, I'm taking a break. I'll be back next week. I'll give you a call when I'm ready."

"What? No! You'll lose your job!" I speak before thinking.

He takes a few quick steps towards me and I think he may hit me, but he doesn't and I'm a little disappointed. He stops short, gritting his teeth. He hisses more than speaks.

"I'm going to be part of something good, and I don't give a shit about this job, you do." He walks back into the house and the bedroom door slams.

Suzy is yelling again, I take a breath and go into the house.

I hold her in the rocker until I hear him in the hall. He comes into the living room, sets his suitcase down and kneels on the floor next to Scott. He rubs his hair and hugs him, softly kissing his forehead and cheeks.

Scott struggles to see the TV and finally looks Carl in the face.

"Daddy's going off for a few days, I have some big things to do. You take care of the girls. I'll bring you something special when I come back."

Scott looks suspiciously at Carl, then looks at the suitcase.

"I like rockets, just so you know." He says with authority, "and sissy likes bunnies."

Carl gives him another kiss and comes over to us.

"Goodbye," he says quietly.

Suzy slides off my lap and toddles to his suitcase, inspecting it.

He kneels down and kisses her head. She tries to climb onto the case. He picks her up and squeezes her, then walks her back to me.

I don't get up.

With a sigh and a wink he's gone.

I feel like I have been punched in the chest. What do we do now?

#

(Present)

My knees hurt from kneeling near the chair in the corner. I've gathered all the things I think will help.

The pile appears like a small shrine in front of me. Collections of tissue, pages ripped from home and garden magazines and a pink stuffed bunny sit carefully placed on the chair. The sunset sends a red glow through the window giving a wild look to the scene.

"Mom?" a slender, green eyed woman approaches from the doorway, "Mom, are you alright? It's Suzy."

I look up, my eyes are wet from tears, "You know he's gone right? What if he never comes back? I pray he'll come back."

"Oh, mom, he'll come back, it'll be okay." Suzy replies squatting next to me. "Let's get up now, this has to be killing your knees."

"You know he's not your father, Suzy. I'm sorry but you're not his real daughter. I'm so sorry," I begin to whimper. A dam is bursting in my chest. "I'm sorry…"

Suzy purses her lips and closes her eyes.

"Mom, get up, let's get up." She says softly and tugs gently on my arms but I don't move.

She stands up and yells toward the door. "Kay! Come here please. I need help."

After a moment of silence, the sound of footsteps bring a winded woman to the door. "Is she okay?"

"Yeah, she's fine, I guess. But she won't get up, can you help me?" Suzy's voice is high and tight.

"Of course. Here, let's try together." The women come in close.

They each grab me under an arm, Suzy's slight bony hands on one side and Kay's firm stable grip on the other.

"On the count of three." Kay counts, "1-2-3!" They both pull up.

But I don't want to get up, I need to finish. I need to stay here.

"Nooo! Oh, leave me. Don't touch me! Leave me here.

Please leave me alone." I go limp, wailing, slipping through their hands. I land with a soft thud and curl up on the floor. The heavy heartache fixes me to the floor.

The women's eyes meet, "I guess we can just leave her for a bit," Kay says cautiously.

Suzy takes a shuddered breath, her voice cracks, "I don't know what other choice we have."

"I mean it's up to you, but let's give her some time."

Suzy pats my hair and whispers, "I'll be back in a minute, Mom."

"Just goooo!" I howl, not sure if I mean it but I don't want to be bothered.

After they leave I roll to my side and cry. I feel hopeless. The effort of figuring out why is too much.

Thoughts cycle through my head telling me I don't deserve anything. I am a burden. I am worthless. I shiver as a coldness washes over me, I will stay here forever.

The man in the black sweatsuit pads across the floor to where I'm curled up. He looks at me for a moment, his slippers are blurry through my tears. He grabs a brightly colored afghan from the back of the chair and lays it over me.

The warmth is immediate. When I turn my head to look at him, he winks and shuffles out the door.

#

9

(September 1963)

Carl has been gone for more than a week with no word.

My mother keeps coming over to ask if I need anything but she doesn't ask about Carl. This means the Ypsi rumor mill must have already filled her in.

I want to ask what she knows and what the rumors are but I'm desperately afraid it's the truth.

The closest thing to information about Carl I've gotten are the news snippets from radio and television about the marches, protests and arrests. I try to scan footage of crowds on T.V. to see if I can catch a glimpse of him but the shadowy images give up nothing.

I can't help but laugh at my newfound attentiveness to current events. Carl has been going on about these things for years but only now am I beginning to understand the magnitude of what's happening.

My mother's sudden presence in my kitchen startles me. I almost drop the plate I've been aggressively scrubbing for the last few minutes. "Mom, I didn't hear you come in."

She gives me a look that stops my hands but doesn't settle my racing heart. "Doris, we need to talk."

My stomach tightens.

I know she's going to talk to me about Carl. I take my time arranging the dishcloth on the edge of the sink and don't respond until I walk to the table and take a seat. "Okay."

"I thought you should know that Carl has been arrested and is in jail, he's in some town called Orangeburg." She searches my face as my emotions parade across it.

"What? How do you know?" The questions spill out as they enter my mind.

"I heard it from your brother, I guess a couple of guys found out because they know some of the coloreds that Carl left with." She leans against the counter with her eyebrows raised, "That's all I know about it Doris. Now I think it's about time you tell me what's going on here."

I continue to stare at her. A flood of worry drowns my brain, I can't find a safe place to begin.

"Okay, let me start then. Carl has obviously left you. Everyone in town is talking about it. There are a few theories as to why. Some of the kinder gossips say he has run off with a negro girl to these rallies. There are rumors that he's doing drugs and run off with some beatniks or hippies. The most popular and most detailed talk is that you had an affair, or many affairs, with Paul..."

She pauses here and I know I must have given something away to confirm this last suspicion because she clears her throat and adds, "I see," before pulling out a chair and taking a seat across from me.

For a brief moment I think she might reach out and comfort me, but she offers neither touch nor words of comfort.

"Doris, Katie Starkweather told everyone in town about how she saw you sneaking out of Paul's truck looking every bit a mess the night of the funeral. You made that woman's year, she finally had something interesting to say."

I get up to find a handkerchief, she waits until I return to my chair before she continues. "I saw you sneak out after him at the VFW and I heard you take your car that night. Who knows who else did. Did you really think you were being clever?"

Having my mother lay it out, only adds to the embarrassment, how could I really have thought no one would know. This town lives and breathes gossip, of course people would remember and discuss it in detail, they'll fill in the blanks with whatever makes the story most interesting.

I put my head on the table and breathe deeply.

"I know, I know... I'm so dumb.... So goddamn stupid, I know!" I pick up my head to look at her.

"I can't undo it, I can't make it better. I would say I'd take it back if I could. I would say it was a mistake, but I don't know if that's true... And it doesn't matter anyhow."

Suzy makes a few noises from her room and I get up to check on her. I get her from the crib and bring her out. My mother looks from me to Suzy and back and shakes her head.

"I guess there are some mistakes too precious to wish you could ever undo."

She takes Suzy from me and kisses her round cheeks. "Oh, little girl, your momma has one fine mess on her hands. But Grandma's here and you're gonna be alright." Suzy grins and grabs a handful of my mother's dark red hair.

I give them a half smile and hope she's right.

#

(Present)

"Are we going home?" I ask Scott from the back seat. We move quickly on the wide multi-lane road and it makes me nervous.

"No, mom. We're going visiting, we're almost there."

"Who are we visiting? I don't know anyone over here?" I'm not really sure where we are but since nothing looks familiar I feel like it's a safe assumption.

"We're looking at a new place for you to stay where you can make new friends. Mom, don't worry." The car starts to slow, "You're going to be alright."

We pull up to a long low brick building that sprawls in two directions from the main structure. The drive pulls up under the covered entrance and loops around to a huge lot. A tall white fence hides the side of the building near the parking lot and low flowered bushes meet the windows on the other side. A few old people sit in wheelchairs near the doors as people in matching green scrubs stare at their phones on the benches.

When Scott comes around to help me get out of the car, I hear a familiar voice. "Mom! I think you are going to love this place." A pretty red haired woman walks up to the car. She reminds me of someone.

"Scott, I've been here for a bit so I started looking around and asking some questions. I'll fill you in later." She slaps Scott on the shoulder and comes in to hug me.

I'm happy to hug the woman, she smells like fabric softener.

"Yeah Suzy, I got caught up, we had some trouble convincing her to come so… sorry we're late." Scott says, sounding more annoyed than sorry.

"My daughter's name is Suzy." I chime in hoping to place the mysterious stranger.

The woman laughs and rolls her eyes at Scott. "Come on, the coordinator is going to show us around."

When we get up to the doors a towering woman in a blue suit comes out and introduces herself as the residential coordinator. I don't even hear her name because I'm so engrossed in her height.

"Whoa, you're a big one!" I say in surprise. The woman laughs and says she gets that a lot. "How tall are you?" I ask because I can't help myself, Scott gives me a look.

"I'm 6'2, and the weather is fine up here." She smirks at her own joke.

We spend a lot of time walking around. The woman is obviously trying to sell us something but I can't figure out what it is. She seems particularly interested in making sure I see the things she points out. I hope Scott tells her I don't have any money.

When we get back to the main lobby she pauses. "We're going to look at our memory care wing now, we need to make sure the doors close behind us when we come in and out of the different areas. It is all part of our security system."

She flips a card in front of a black box and pulls open one of two heavy double doors. The room on the other side is heavily furnished with bulky couches and recliners. A few grey haired ladies are scattered amongst the furniture. Two have their heads down, chins resting on their chests and a couple more are engrossed in the program on the television. The lone man in the group is leaning against a wood beam making clicking noises with his teeth.

"Good afternoon," the woman leading our group chirps to the crowd.

Only one of the ladies looks up, "Oh, wow, you are a big one!" she exclaims when she sees our guide. I take a good look at the woman and have to agree. "My goodness, how tall are you?" I ask before I can stop myself.

The tall woman smiles, "I'm 6'2, and the weather is fine up here."

As we continue our tour, workers in matching scrubs push carts or wheelchairs through the long corridors.

Most of the doors to the rooms are open. We walk through a small room with a large window that overlooks a grassy area scattered with bird baths and feeders. The woman points out a large mounted TV, an adjustable bed that looks like it belongs in a hospital and a small bathroom that includes a monstrous tub with a door in the side.

Suzy steps in and sits in the tub, "Look mom, you will just love this tub." I can't remember the last time I sat in a bathtub but I nod politely.

At the end of the tour we sit in a small cafeteria with coffee and cookies. Scott and Suzy discuss all the programs the place offers, its room sizes and staff. They keep asking me if I like it and their faces want me to say yes, so I do. "It's very nice." I reassure them.

I swirl the last of the coffee in my cup and watch the light and dark make circles in the bottom.

"Why don't you take the mug home as a momento Doris?" says someone from the table. I don't look up but tilt the mug sideways and check out the logo on the side.

A large green tree sprawls over the words "Cicada Grove Senior Community and Memory Care."

There are papers and handshakes exchanged, everyone is talking and stands up at once so I follow suit.

"I'll see you in two weeks, Doris. I know you'll like it here." Says the tallest woman I have ever seen, as she shakes my hand vigorously. I nod reflexively to match the enthusiasm in her voice.

"Sure," I say and stare up at the woman. "How tall are you

anyway?"

#

Past (September 1963)

The deafening hum of cicadas quiets my brain as I sit swirling sweet red wine in a coffee cup.

Lately, after the kids are asleep anxiety washes over me, flooding my mind with questions until it's hard to breathe. Tonight, I thought I would try to drown it before it drowned me.

The lightness of the tapping at the back door startles me as much as an explosion. I'm stuck to my seat, my heart races, did I lock the door? Who would come to the back door? The smolder of twilight through the windows only adds foreboding, but the tapping persists.

Maybe Carl is back. The thought of Carl brings a flame of excitement and hope. The idea carries courage with it, releasing me from my chair and I walk softly to the back door to peek through the window.

I don't see anyone, just my backyard and the eerie brightness of the sheets I forgot to bring in from the line. Then I notice the shadow sitting on the step.

At first I think it *is* Carl and I start to unlock the door, but when the figure turns, the moonlight exposes his light hair and his green eyes glow like a cat's in the darkness.

I pull the door open and stare at him through the screen before I find my voice. "What are you doing here?" I whisper as firmly and angry as I can. So many emotions rushing forward, but fear of waking the kids keeps me from cursing him out. Why is he doing this to me?

"Let me in before someone sees me." Paul says calmly. Not waiting for a reply, he opens the screen door and slides past me.

Casually, he strides down the hall and stands near the kitchen table until I catch up to him.

"Paul, really, what are you doing here?" I ask, scurrying to close the curtains in the dining room.

"I heard Carl left. I happened to be in town, and well... we never got to finish talking."

He says as if this explains anything. I see a faint smile playing on his full lips. Does he think this is funny? He walks slowly around the table, taking in the details of my house. His fingers drag across the backs of the chairs. I keep my distance and lean against the refrigerator.

He looks me in the eyes but I can't read him.

"Doris, can we please just talk?"

Paul pulls out a chair and sits. He leans back and holds his hands up, "Just talking, really... My God, you know I would never hurt you."

My emotions are strong and my throat is tight. I feel like I owe him a conversation, but I know he doesn't belong here. I hate hurting him but I'm so mad at him. I miss him but I miss Carl. I realize how much things have changed.

"I am afraid of you." I blurt without planning to, without moving from my spot, without making a decision.

Paul looks hurt, then laughs softly. His smile changes and I see the Paul who listened to all my troubles years ago, the Paul who was going to save me, the Paul who was really the only person who knew me in this lonely town.

I take the chair farthest from him and sit. He breathes deep, looks at the wine bottle and coffee cup. "Celebrating?"

"Hardly" I say and exhale loudly. I didn't realize I was holding my breath. "Can I get you a cup?" I ask and shake the mug at him.

"I'm not much for wine, I'd take a beer or settle for water. It's so damn hot..."

I get a glass of water and drop a couple ice cubes in it. Neither of us speak until I sit down and pour more wine in my mug. I've been so scared and alone this past week, just being with someone who knows the truth is a relief.

"I know what you want to talk about but I don't know what to say, so you'll have to start." I say breaking the silence.

"I'm not sure either I suppose." He pokes at the ice cubes, watching them bob down under the water.

A few more minutes of silence pass as we occasionally look each other over. It's not tense, even though we're both anticipating and measuring out our next words. The weight of the consequences of our last meeting keep us grounded.

There is so much on the table between us.

"It seems like so long ago that we were together. You know, since it was me and you." Paul runs his hands through his thick blonde hair. "What happened? Why didn't it work? I thought we had a plan?"

The questions are not pleading. His eyes are honest and direct. I realize we never really talked about why we broke up or why I left that night.

When we were together, after the funeral, we didn't talk about anything real. It was all pretend and fantasy, at least for me, no questions.

"I'm sorry Paul."

He rolls his eyes.

"You deserve an explanation. I don't think I could have given you one then, when we were teenagers, but looking back I think I just needed someone here.

My family is so," I have to pause here because the lump in

my throat has returned. I swallow hard and take a long drink of wine. "They are so fucked up, so needy. I used you to stay sane. When you were gone I needed someone here, and you weren't.

Then there was Carl, he was different and I got to be someone new… It just wasn't going to work with us. That's all I guess."

I avoid his gaze, I don't want to know if he's hurt. The wine is making my face warm.

I realize I'm wearing my slippers, and I had taken off my bra long ago. I hope the light fabric of my summer dress is enough to keep me modest. I cross my arms over my chest and slide lower in my chair.

When I look up, Paul is studying me. It only makes me more self conscious.

"Doris, I know we were kids. We had no idea what was coming, but I really loved you, I still do. I don't know how you didn't know I needed you. You didn't even give me a chance…" He takes a deep breath and watches the curtain list in the breeze.

"You were a part of me, of every decision I made and you still are. In my heart you're waiting for me. I just can't figure out how to get back to you."

The weight in my chest is so heavy I'm sure my heart will stop. I'm two women, one who knows Carl is everything I have and the other who can't give up Paul because he still sees me as worthy of everything he has.

The truth is that Paul isn't wrong, I have always been waiting for him.

Good, loyal Paul saves me in all my fantasies of running away. He saves me from this town and all it knows about me He saves me from my father who destroyed my family, he saves me from pretending I'm someone I'm not.

He knows me enough to realize that I still need him to save me, and I know him enough to know that he wants to be the hero.

My breath quickens with the pace of the thoughts in my mind. Paul leans forward and touches my hand. I feel heat spread from his touch to the ache in my heart. I close my eyes and hear Paul's chair scoot on the linoleum floor. When I open my eyes he is just far enough away that I will have to go to him. My body wants me to stand, my heart is torn.

The beginning whimpers of Suzy from her crib rouse my brain from the fuzz of fantasy and back to my real life.

"Suzy." I whisper as I duck away through the kitchen. When I get to her room she's fine, rolled over and is fast asleep in her pink pajamas. I lean over and push her pink bunny away from her face. I feel Paul in the room behind me. He walks softly to the crib and stares down at Suzy. He touches her cheek then her soft red hair. I gently push his arm back.

I don't want him to touch her. I don't want her to be his. Paul may know where I come from, but that is not where I am anymore.

He is no longer the hero, he is the threat. This isn't about us anymore, it's about them.

I lead Paul out of the nursery and close the door. When we reach the kitchen again, he takes my hand. "Could she be mine?" I see the hope in his face.

"No, she's not yours Paul. Please believe me."

He studies me for a moment, still holding my hand.

I wonder if he's going to try to kiss me.

I wonder if I'll let him.

I wonder if I can say no even though I need to.

He drops my hand and sighs, "I can't do this Doris. You have a real family. I'm not going to be the guy who ruins that. *I* wanted this with you." He nods to the house in general, "But I'm not going to push my way in and steal it from someone else."

Feelings of panic and relief make it hard for me to find words. Is he going to leave? Is the decision made? Will Paul and I really be over?

I manage a nod and a half smile before the tears come. I cover my face and lean on the wall. I don't want to cry but I can't help it. It's all too much. I can't stand anymore. I slide down the wall and hug my knees to my chest.

Paul sits down beside me and shoves his handkerchief into my hand. I give up trying to stop the tears and just let go. It's not just a sad cry, I cry with every emotion. All the ones I've held in over the past months come flooding out in uncontrolled, unladylike, mucus drenched sobs. Paul doesn't say anything, he doesn't touch me, he just sits close enough to me that I can feel that he's there.

When I finally finish, I'm afraid to raise my head. I know I'll look horrible. My face is swollen and sticky, but inside there is lightness. There is a tiny spark of optimism, although I can't say for what. After a couple of shuttering, deep breaths I lift my head from my hands. Paul helps me up and holds me in a deep hug for a moment.

"Whatever you need Doris, I'll be here." He whispers and kisses the top of my head.

I know he means it, I know he is asking me if I want him to wait. I know if I nod and say nothing he will stay in the shadows of my life waiting to save me forever. I know that if I keep him there then I will continue to need saving. I squeeze him tighter.

"I know Paul," I pull away from him and look into his eyes. "I need you to move on. I need you to let go, I'll be okay, and so will you. Please…"

I will be okay, I repeat to myself.

I take his hand and lead him to the back door. His eyes linger at Suzy's doorway when we pass.

"Paul," I whisper to make him look at me. "Find someone else to make you happy, someone who deserves you. You're so good…"

He clears his throat and barely whispers,"But you don't know… you deserve…"

His voice fades, he searches my face and runs his fingers along my cheek. His eyes look longingly into mine. I want to look away, but I don't want to leave any doubt.

He leans down and kisses me softly on the lips. I linger there for just a moment, a goodbye kiss. Neither of us lean in for more.

He slips out the door in silence. I watch his shadow pass in front of the forgotten sheets until he blends seamlessly into the dark. The clock loudly ticks away the seconds from the kitchen. I exhale one last shuddering breath then lock the door.

#

10

(Present)

The doctor slides a sheet of paper across the table to me. "Mrs. Atkins, can you draw a clock?"

"Why sure, of course." I reply and stare at the large empty circle printed on the paper. The word clock bounces around in my brain but I can't picture the thing.

"Here's a pen Mom." Suzy hands me the pen from the table.

After a few seconds I draw a large line down the middle of the circle. I know there should be numbers, so I add the numbers 4 and 9 to the left of the line.

It doesn't seem right but it's the best I can come up with. I toss the pen back on the desk and lean forward in my chair. I stare at the dark skin of my doctor, appreciating the depth of the tone. He reaches for my drawing and turns it a few times as if he can't decide which way it goes.

"You know I insisted on having a colored doctor because I believe that we're all equal." I declare with pride.

"Mother! I am so sorry Dr. Davis." Suzy sits up straight, giving the dark skinned physician her best "we're not racist, really" smile.

Her obvious embarrassment irritates me.

"What? I just wanted him to know that Carl and I support the colored people." I lean on the table toward Dr. Davis. "Did you know Carl saw the man speak? He went to the marches to see him, you know, *the* guy." I try to find the man's name as my hands fly all over attempting to mime the word.

"Dr. King, you mean?" Dr. Davis suggests, trying to suppress a smile.

"Yes, the King! That's him!" I slap the desk hard with my hand. I knew the name, I could see it.

"My father was an activist when he was young," Suzy speaks rapidly now. "So that's what she's talking about. He really did go to the March on Washington though. He always was proud of that."

Suzy presses her hands together. "My mother really wouldn't have used the word colored, you know, it's just the…"

Dr. Davis lets the smile spread across his face. "Yes, of course I know. People have said a lot worse here, about me and about people they love, so don't worry about it." The doctor looks at his clipboard then turns to me.

"Now Mrs. Atkins, I'm going to say five words and I want you to repeat them back to me when I'm done. Are you ready? Apple, Table…."

I'm already annoyed with the game, I notice a string is loose on the hem of my shirt.

"Can you repeat any of the words back to me Doris?"

I look up to see the Doctor staring back at me with raised eyebrows. "Can you tell me any of the words from the list?"

"I don't think so," I breathe heavily and look at my watch. "Are we almost done here?"

"It's not a great day for her," Suzy announces to the doctor, ignoring my question. "Yesterday she was on it. If you didn't know her you might not even guess there was anything wrong. But today, ehh, it's not a good day."

"What are you talking about, I'm just fine today. As good as I was yesterday. I don't even know why I am at the doctors, I feel great." I'm flustered, my eyes start to water.

"Well, you know it will go like that." Dr. Davis replies without looking at me. "Let's take her down to the lab for another blood draw. We will check her B12 levels and run a few other screens."

The two of them exchange knowing looks. Suzy pats my hand.

Dr. Davis stands and opens the door. I grab my jacket and bustle out into the hallway.

"Check out with Mary, here's your lab slip. Have a nice day Mrs. Atkins." He hands her a yellow paper then walks the opposite direction.

Suzy starts to shoo me along the hallway.

"I'm not going anywhere until you tell me why I'm here. I am not a child!" I stomp my foot to keep from crying. "Why is he drawing my blood? I'm not sick!"

Suzy closes her eyes and breathes deeply. "Mom, I'm sorry, this is just a check up. It's routine blood draws. The older you get the more tests they run."

She doesn't look directly at me when she says this, her eyes focus somewhere behind me. It makes me uneasy.

The image of a lab slip pops into my mind, I start to pat my pockets. "Now just let me see where I put it."

"Mom, I have your things here, look. Take your purse." Suzy hangs the bag over my shoulder. "Come on."

I follow a few steps behind her through a blue door

marked "Lab." A young tech with bright red hair in a high pony-tail greets us. "Do you have your lab slip?"

"Sure do." I flop my large purse on the counter. "Let me see, it's here somewhere." I rummage through the sack.

"Mom, I've got it. It's right here" Suzy hands the tech a yellow paper.

"There's so much stuff in here!" I take out handfuls of tissues and paper and pile it on the counter.

"Mom, I gave her the slip, you don't have one" Suzy hisses as she tries to stuff the litter back into my purse.

"No, no, Suzy, I've got it here somewhere." I know I have the slip. I can see it in my mind, Suzy's interference is making me lose the picture. "Just let me do it!" I snap.

"Um, is this okay for a minute," Suzy makes big eyes and crinkles her nose at the tech. I glare at her. "She might have to just do this for a bit before we can move on."

"Sure, do what you got to do. We'll call her back in a minute." The tech shrugs and disappears somewhere behind a partition.

"Mom, I'll be over here, when you're done." Suzy plops herself down in the nearest chair.

"Fine!"

I pick up a handful of wrappers from my purse and crinkle them in my fist. The thought is gone. I know I was doing something. I'm left with the unsatisfying feeling that something is incomplete.

"Doris?" A young man calls from the doorway.

I look at the mess, then at Suzy helplessly. She gets up and shovels handfuls of the refuse back into my bag.

"Okay mom," Suzy leads me to the door. "That's us."

"Is this Doris then?" He points to me. "What is your birth date ma'am?"

I'm distracted by his dark features. "June 18th."

The man gives a questioning look to Suzy as they walk to the chair. "Sorry, she has Alzheimer's, she doesn't really remember. It's March 25th."

"I know my own birthday, Suzy." I give her an annoyed look.

"OK, sorry mom." She squeezes my hand and looks at the man. "Can we get moving with this, it's been a long day."

The tech rolls up my sleeve and prepares the tourniquet, "Ok, this might pinch for a minute."

His dark fingers wrap firmly around my forearm.

"You know, I always request a colored doctor, I want to make sure you all get a fair shot."

The man raises his eyebrows and looks at Suzy.

"Sorry," Suzy groans, rubbing her forehead. "It's been a really long day."

#

(September 1963)

"Yes sir, thank you very much."

I hang the phone gently on it's cradle and plop down at the table.

"It's gonna be awhile before anything happens. Their lawyer says they're holding him for destroying public property and picketing in an area with an anti-picketing ordinance."

My mother raises an eyebrow. "I can't see Carl destroying anything, this is crazy."

"I know. Apparently an officer saw him rip a 'coloreds only' sign from a drinking fountain at some public building. He was arrested with a bunch of others. The jail is so full they're moving him to another county. The lawyer said they're swamped but if we had $100 we could get him out."

My mother stands up to dig her cigarettes out of her purse and fumbles for a minute before she gets one lit.

"Did you tell him you don't have $100 because Carl quit his job to go marching around America for colored people?"

"Even if we did he still couldn't leave South Carolina legally, but the lawyer said no one would look for him if he left."

"Just great, he'd be a fugitive. Fine mess..." My mother yanks open the refrigerator and rummages around.

"Did you tell him you got kids to feed? Bills to pay? I mean $100?"

She finds some wine in the fridge and pours two full coffee mugs, they clink together as she carries them to the table in one hand so she can hold her lit cigarette with the other.

Drops of red slosh over the edge of the white mug she plunks down in front of me. I take a long drink. It's a little sweet but mostly bitter, especially since I'm not accustomed to drinking before noon.

"No Mom, he didn't seem too interested in my troubles. I don't think he expects us to send money. He said Carl would be writing. I guess we just have to wait."

She isn't listening to my answer, she's back in the kitchen running water, banging dishes in the sink and muttering to herself.

"Fine mess...$100..."

I bring my half full mug to the sink and shoo her away before she chips every dish we own. "Why don't you go check on the kids and I'll do these."

She picks up the cigarette she had teetering at the edge of the sink and takes a drag.

"Please, go find the kids?"

"Fine."

She's yelling before she even gets to the hall. "Who wants to help Grandma with the leaves in the backyard!" She's answered by squeals and the pounding of uncoordinated feet running to the back door.

I squeeze a little soap into the hot water and swish my hands around to suds it up. She's right. What are we going to do if Carl isn't bringing home any money?

I hadn't been sure he was going to stay here when he came back but I assumed he would make sure the bills were paid.

I know we still have some money in the bank from his mother, probably enough for one or two house payments. I also have Carl's last check from the factory that came in the mail but I'm not sure if the bank will let me cash it. Barbara Lemon, the head teller at the bank, would just love to tell everyone that I came in begging them to let me cash my runaway husband's check.

Ugh, no way.

I begin to scrub harder on the pan from last night's potatoes. So, we would need maybe ten dollars a week for food and milk, then money for the electric bill and gas for the car. I wish I knew for sure how much was in the bank. Anxiety makes my stomach churn.

I need a real plan. I pull the plug from the bottom of the sink and leave the half washed dishes.

"Hey Mom, can you stay with the kids a bit? I need to run into town for a minute." I yell out the back door. She nods and the kids wave from the small pile of leaves they've made.

I try to run a brush through my hair before I go but it's a lost cause so I tie a scarf around the mess and call it good.

At the bank, I manage to get our account balance from a smug looking Barbara without her asking any nosey questions. I sit in the parking lot and stare at the number. It's too small.

Our mortgage payment is due in two weeks and this will barely cover it. What are we going to live on? I guess I'll need to get a job. My mother or David could probably watch the kids while I worked. I haven't worked since I was pregnant with Scott at the sewing shop.

I close my eyes and breathe.

I am going to take care of this.

I am really on my own, there's no else to save us.

I walk over to the gas station and get a paper. I search the ads for something I can do.

There are a few postings for GM factory work, which would probably pay well but I don't know any women who work on a factory floor. The Chick Inn has a waitress job, there's a typist position and a small ad for a receptionist for the local dentist. I don't have experience for any of these jobs.

There's no sense in waiting, I tell myself. I know the factory offices are open and I figure I'll start where the pay is the best.

When I arrive at the Willow Run plant, it takes me a few minutes to find the right entrance.

The receptionist looks me over and I become conscious of what I'm wearing. It's not bad, I think, as I try to smooth out its front. It's a plaid print dress that I made myself with a white collar and tiny white rose buttons down the front. The scarf on my head is a solid rust color that almost blends in with my hair.

I realize I have no idea what I should be wearing to look for work at a factory, or anywhere else really.

"So you want to apply to work *out* in the factory?" the elderly receptionist asks without hiding her confusion.

"Yes, ma'am." I reply with as much confidence as I can muster.

"Are you one of those women's rights girls or something?" She scowls as she rifles through the papers on her desk. "Have you ever worked in a factory?"

"No, I just would like to work. I'm a hard worker and I don't mind getting my hands dirty." The receptionist looks at my hands as if she actually expects them to be dirty.

"The ad in the paper said you were hiring at this plant, right?" I smile and try not to sound impatient. I start to wonder if she's ever going to tell me how I can apply for the job. Just then a young man comes in and approaches the receptionist.

"Excuse me ma'am," He takes off his hat. "I am inquiring about the job you have posted in the newspaper?"

The receptionist smiles at the man then eyes me suspiciously. "You both can have a seat over there, I'll get someone to help you."

She leaves her desk and slowly makes her way down the hall. A few minutes later she returns.

"Young man, you can come back here, Mr. Hawkins will see you now. It's the first door on the right." She points towards the hallway.

"And we'll have you fill out this application. I'll give you a call if a position opens up that meets your, uh, qualifications." She flashes a false smile as she slides a sheet of paper across the desk towards me.

I start to reach for the paper, then stop.

"No. I'll wait here to see Mr. Hawkins."

"Miss I don't think you understand, Mr. Hawkins is busy and he asked that you fill out an application, then we can call you later."

I notice the nameplate on the front of the woman's desk reads Gladys Buttrice.

"Mrs. Buttrice, I know you just sent that other man back there to talk to Mr. Hawkins. I was here first but I will wait to be interviewed."

I'm surprised by my own insistence, I wasn't even sure I wanted a factory job but this whole situation has me annoyed.

Gladys makes a guttural sound and makes her way down the hall again. When she returns she sits at her desk and types aggressively for a few moments before she speaks to me.

"Mr. Hawkins will come fetch you himself when he's ready. I suggest you fill out the application. It could be awhile."

I've just finished the application when the young man who had come in after me emerges from the hallway. He gives a half grimace that I take as an attempt at a smile as he makes his way to the door.

A few minutes later a short man with a few desperate black hairs left to cover his pink scalp comes out followed by a trail of smoke from his cigarette. He leans on one hand over Gladys and she nods in my direction. I sit up straight but don't attempt a smile. He strikes me as the type that might think smiling is a waste of time.

"You finished with your paperwork Miss?" It isn't as much a question as a command, his voice is loud, almost a shout.

"Yes sir, I have it here." I stand up and take a few steps forward. I don't hand him the paper for fear it's my only ticket to the interview and I don't want to lose it.

He starts back toward the hallway and yells over his shoulder, "Alright then, come on back."

I follow him in without looking at Gladys. The hall is short with only two other doors besides the one labeled for Mr. Hawkins. One is labeled "private" and the other, at the end of the hall, has a variety of signs and warnings on it but the most prominent labels it "Production Floor."

Mr. Hawkins sits down and waves for me to do the same. The office is small and smokey with a large window and a half dozen filing cabinets. Once I sit down, Mr. Hawkins motions for me to give him the application.

"Now Miss, er, Mrs. Atkins, why do you want to work here? I see you're a married woman, don't you have children?" His voice has softened to a normal volume and he doesn't seem as intimidating as before.

"Well, sir, my husband is not able to work right now and we have bills to pay." I pause, trying to figure out where I'm going from here with the story.

"I know this factory is a good job and I'm a good worker so I think it's a good fit…. And I have two children, sir."

Mr. Hawkins leans back in his chair, staring at me. He breathes with his mouth slightly open, making a low whistle when he inhales. The room is filled with the sound of his whistle and the rumble of the work beyond the walls.

"So what do you want to do, exactly? Do you want to work on the line with all the men? Do you want to work in the office? I'm having a hard time here." He trails off but is still studying me.

I sit up as straight as I can and answer before I've really finished the thought in my head.

"I plan to work on the line sir, I will work with whoever is out there. My husband had worked on the line in Detroit for a few years. I've heard stories. I know it's repetitive, long and fast paced work. I can manage all that. I just need a good job and I'll be a loyal employee."

Mr. Hawkins taps his desk for a moment before he stands up and grabs a long grey jacket from a hook behind the door. "Let's have you put this on and follow me. We're gonna get this figured out, but that dress isn't gonna work on the floor."

I slide the jacket on, it hangs past my knees, then follow him into the hall and through the door with all the extra warning notices on it.

Immediately the noise overwhelms me, I resist the urge to cover my ears. I hurry to follow Mr. Hawkins quick steps.

There are cars dangling from the ceiling as men move underneath them with parts and tools. The cars move slowly and continuously like a parade of ghostly skeletons.

We pass through another set of doors and the cars here are on the floor. They straddle a huge trench as they continue their slow march on tracks. These cars look more complete, I recognize them as the Corvair. As they inch along, I see men working both under them and alongside them, making small adjustments to the headlights and checking over the vehicles.

Mr. Hawkins bellowing voice doesn't seem so alarming in here. This area is quieter than the last but is still loud, full of buzzing and low hums from the machines.

"This is the area we're hiring for, you have to pay attention, be quick and make sure your area of inspection is right on. Guys get real mad when you point out their mistakes but you can't let mistakes go by, they got to be fixed. If they get to the customer it's on you."

He lights up a cigarette and starts walking toward a tall skinny man with a clipboard. "Hey, Lee, you mind if you had to work with a lady out here?"

The man turns around, glances quickly in my direction then shrugs. "You got a Rosie the Riveter here or something?" He chuckles to himself and shakes his head. "It don't bother me as long as we don't have to stop if she breaks a nail." His shoulders shake up and down as he chuckles deeper at his own joke.

"Alright, keep working Lee, I'll talk to you in a bit." Mr. Hawkins continues through a small grey door, I follow obediently. We pass through some grey brick hallways then out into the parking lot. I see my car in the distance.

"Okay, so we can give this a try if it's what you want to do. My sister works in a factory in Detroit so I don't have any problems with ladies in the shop. Most of the women who work in the factory here do the sewing, it's been awhile since we've had a lady on the line." He pauses to give me a look. "And since you're a married woman I'm assuming you won't cause any trouble?"

"Trouble?" I say and stare back at him a second before I get his meaning. "No, I'm a family woman, no trouble."

"Good, we don't need any distractions. You show up on Monday, keep your hair up and wear some pants. You might want to get some work boots too."

I look down at my canvas shoes and feel a little ridiculous. I take off his jacket and hand it to him.

He tucks it under his arm and continues, "I'll have someone here to train you and the other new guy. Does that sound good?"

I nod and shake his hand. "Thanks." I say, and risk giving him a smile. After he walks back into the building I mutter to myself "What did I just sign up for?"

#

11

"Do you want to keep those Mom, or can they go to storage?"

Suzy kneels on the floor in front of me surrounded by shoes. I hold a heavy pair of brown leather work boots, they're scuffed and worn. They feel familiar but I can't place them. I can't imagine what I would need them for.

I bend down to try them on my feet.

Suzy takes them from me and tosses them into a box that says "storage unit." I don't want them in the box. She picks up a pair of penny loafers and inspects them. She looks at me for a moment like she's going to ask me a question then tosses the shoes in the box.

"Scott should be here any minute to help. Why don't you go and see if you can help Kay until he gets here."

I stand up and walk, carefully weaving around the boxes in the room. When I get to the door I see the man in black duck into the room next door. I push on the half closed door, it slides with resistance, like something's behind it. The room is long with a large armoire blocking part of the view. Boxes are scattered and piled through this room as well.

"Doris, where are you going?" Someone asks loudly from behind me. "Why don't you come out here so you don't trip over anything and get hurt. We don't need any accident reports on your last day!"

Kay grabs my elbow and gently guides me out of the doorway. I don't want to go with her. There was something I was looking for before she came in. I pull my elbow away and try to step back toward the door.

"Now Doris, come on, that isn't your room, and it's moving day. Let's go to the kitchen." She tries guiding me by the hips.

"No, I want to go this way." I say in a whisper. Where did my voice go? I try again, "I want to go this way!" But still my voice is quiet and cracks.

"What Doris? Honey, I think you're tired, let's go have a seat and I can get you some coffee. Would you like some coffee?" Kay's voice gets higher with the word coffee and the expression on her face makes me feel like she is offering a treat to a dog.

"No!" I manage to yell this word louder than I expected as I push Kay's hands off of me. She steps back and takes a deep breath.

"Let's not be difficult, Doris. You can't stand here in the hallway, you HAVE to move…" She's interrupted by a knock from another room. "I'll be back, maybe that's your son and he can help us."

She walks briskly down the hall and disappears around the corner. I stare after her.

My eyes trail along the wall to a group of framed Saturday Evening Post covers.

One is of a boy and a policeman sitting at a soda fountain, another is of a boy with his arm around a girl on a bench. The one of a woman in overalls holding a sandwich and a heavy piece of machinery captures my attention. I search my brain for a thought that keeps slipping away.

"She's right here. I don't know if you can get her to come

out of the hallway but I haven't had any luck." Kay says to some-one out of view before she continues in the other direction.

Scott peeks his head around the corner and smiles at me.

"Scott!" I say and clap my hands. He comes in for a hug. "Have you seen this?" I say and point to the magazine cover of the woman.

"Yes, Mom, it's you, 'Rosie the Riveter." He squeezes my hand. "Remember when we used to call you that?"

I nod because it rings true somewhere in my mind but I can't really find the memory. Is that really me? The almost-memory makes me smile.

I loop my arm cheerfully through Scotts and lean my head on him. "Let's get some coffee."

#

(September 1963)

I'm so tired that my fingers refuse to cooperate as I fumble with the laces on my black leather boots. My arms and shoulders ache, the hum and beep of the assembly line still keeps rhythm in my head. It's only my third day but I'm not sure I'll last the week.

"Momma!" Scott runs full speed down the hall to greet me with a bear hug that I can't return with any strength.

"Oh, little man, were you good for grandma?" I kiss his forehead.

Scott screws up one side of his face and taps his chin with his finger, "I think so. But not Sissy, she took out all of grandmas' knitting and mixed it up everywhere."

Just then my mother and Suzy emerge from the hallway. Suzy toddles into my arms and I pull her on my lap. "Were you a little stinker for grandma today?" I ask with a smile, she giggles and cuddles into me.

"They are always angels." My mother says, as she gathers her things. "I started the soup on the stove, it just needs about ten more minutes."

"Thanks, do you want to stay for dinner?" It is both a polite question and a plea.

My mother refuses with a smile. "I'll need to check on your brother, he might starve if I don't remind him to eat."

It's not even 4 o'clock and I'm ready for bed. I don't know how I'll make it three more hours until the kids bedtime. Thank God for television I think to myself.

Scott has already returned to the T.V. I carry Suzy with me to check the soup. It smells amazing and my stomach agrees loudly. I take crackers from the cupboard, and share one with Suzy.

A letter on the table makes me catch my breath. The handwriting is small but dramatic, *Mrs. Doris Atkins*, it's from Carl. I hand Suzy two crackers and push her towards the living room.

This is my first contact with Carl directly since he left. I feel hopeful and anxious, like when we first met. There's a return address for the jail in the corner. I open it to find a single sheet of plain paper.

Dear Doris,

I'm sorry to have gotten myself here. I hope you and the kids are getting by alright. I miss you all so much.

I know this is hard and it's a bad circumstance - but it's for a good cause. I hope these South Carolina judges come around soon. The jail they moved me to isn't as crowded as the last but it's not any friendlier. Even though I'm white, I'm the disgust of many here for being on the side of negroes. One guy insisted on being moved from my cell because he said he may "kill the nigger lover." I admit I'm scared but take solace knowing I'm on the right side.

I feel more like me than I have in awhile.

If something does happen to me, I hope my children can be proud that their father was fighting for something right. I hope you would be proud.

I'm sorry we left things badly. I haven't stopped loving you, I want you to know that.

I'm still angry and confused. I struggle with knowing what we really have, and what I thought we had. I feel much like the beach-comber in the Sylvia Plath poem. I'm not sure if there is anything real for us together, mostly because I don't know if there was ever any-thing real on your part.

Did I actually know your love? Maybe it was just my hope that you loved me as I love you? I know that I only want what is real from now on. Please take time and think about that. Be honest and kind when you consider a future with me. I don't want to be needed, I only need to be wanted and loved.

No matter what, I will make sure you are all taken care of when I return. Please forgive me for not being able to now.

Love for you all,

Carl

Tears fall and stain the paper. I do want him to love me. I want him to come back. I want things to be different, how they should have been all along. I should have appreciated his heart and appreciated who he was.

An image of our perfect family drifts into my head, the four of us, all tidy and happy. I want that image because it seems simple, everyone has a role, everyone fits. It's what I thought "normal" families had. It's what I think I've always wanted.

Now I know that isn't right for Carl, but is it right for me?

Carl says he wants what is real and, although he's tried, he won't fit his role. What does that mean for us? His question is no longer simple and I just don't have the energy right now to figure out the answer.

Tears continue to fall as I fold the letter and tuck it into the envelope. An excerpt from the Sylvia Plath "Two Lovers and a Beachcomber" poem and his mailing address are on the back. *"We are not what we might be..."*

It's so like Carl to leave everything up to a poem and make it feel like a riddle. Isn't that the sort of thing I loved about him when we met? I can't remember when that part of him disappeared, or when I stopped noticing.

I stick the letter in the cupboard next to the spices and stir the soup. The smell wafts upward and my stomach growls loudly. My tired hand shakes as it grasps the spoon. The fatigue and my senses keep me grounded here, in this moment, in what is real.

#

(Present)

My eyes can only find a white expanse before me. I continue to blink and stare into the abyss. Distant voices and a buzzing sound fill my ears, anxiety creeps into my chest. Slowly the white becomes the ripple of sheets. My eyes focus. I'm lying on my side. I consider rolling to my back but as I think about the movement my anxiety builds. I feel like I may roll off the bed. I'm not sure if there's something there to catch me when I roll backwards.

There's a tremor on my stomach. I realize it's my own hand, I slide it unsteadily into view. It looks old and foreign. The knuckles are swollen and blue veins bulge out in maze-like patterns, impossible to follow with the shaking.

The dark line where the white wall and white sheet meet

is both orienting and frightening. Where am I? If I could just roll over maybe I could figure it out, but fear keeps me in place.

A few muscles twitch and my knees knock together. My trembling hand lifts in front of me and starts to move down, up over my hip and behind me. I can see the movement but it doesn't register as under my command. My hand lands on a solid surface and slowly brings the rest of my body with it. I exhale in relief when I realize I am safe, and lying on my back.

The white ceiling is unremarkable. I look to the left and see a familiar looking recliner, a colorful afghan and stuffed bunny rest on the back of it. A small table is squeezed between the edge of the bed and the recliner. A long window with a deep sill glows brightly next to the chair. There are rectangles silhouetted on the sill in varying sizes. I notice two doors in the room, they are exactly the same and mirror each other on either wall. There is a small hallway that leads out of my sight.

When I look toward my feet I see I'm fully dressed, down to my canvas tennis shoes. Maybe I'm going somewhere. Maybe I am going home. My shoes wiggle in agreement. I push myself up onto my elbows and lower my feet, one at a time, over the edge of the bed to the floor.

I make my way to the door near the window, when I open it I find a small closet stuffed full of clothing and boxes. I pull out a couple of shirts, they look like they would be mine. I need to pack up if I'm going to check out. I see a small suitcase at the bottom of the closet under a mass of purses and bags. When I've stuffed as much as I can into the suitcase I struggle to zip it and leave a few things peeking out.

On my way out the stuffed bunny catches my eye and I tuck it in the crook of my arm before I pull open the large door.

It opens to a wide hallway with dark wood floors stretching in both directions. I see a red exit sign over a heavy metal door at one end of the hall. In the other direction, a few more doors line the hall between me and what looks like the hotel lobby. I walk slowly toward the lobby, pulling my suitcase is awkward but it isn't far. A young man in a polo style shirt and a gold name tag walks briskly towards me.

"Young man, can you take my bag to the car while I check out."

He gives me a wide smile. "Sure Ma'am, I'll take your bag. Why don't you have a seat here while I get someone to help you." He points me toward a large flower print sofa. I don't see a check-out counter so I follow his direction and wait. The huge television mounted on the wall has an "I Love Lucy" program blaring loudly. I notice another woman sitting near me in a chintz patterned armchair.

"I love this program!" I yell to her over the commercial break. The woman looks at me suspiciously.

I smile at her and point to the television. She looks from me to the television and back. She says a few words but they sound like gibberish, so I try again.

"This one is funny!" I yell at the woman. She points a crooked finger at the television and starts to laugh.

I'm confused about her laughter. The television has a fluffy looking teddy bear bouncing in a clothes basket. I don't know, maybe it is funny, but that bear is at least cute. I notice I'm holding a pink stuffed bunny in my elbow and I put it on my lap. I bounce it like the bear on the television. I give a little chuckle and settle back into the couch. Yeah, this bear is funny.

I wonder what's on next.

#

12

My first check from the factory is $65. This is more than I made in a month working at the fabric shop. I'm only working about 25 hours a week but this will be enough to keep us moving. I stop at the bank, then the grocery store.

The kids and I are both tired of soup. I splurge on a whole chicken and figure that once I roast it, the three of us will have dinner for the week. As I load up the car I mentally check our financial status. I still have $40 left from my check and the mortgage has already been paid this month. I haven't called on our other bills to see when they are due, but nothing has come in the mail yet so for now I think we're fine.

A small but electric feeling of hope begins in my chest. It replaces the fear that has been there in the weeks since Carl left.

We may just make it. We may be okay and it's because of me.

I did it.

A few tears of relief and pride slide down my cheeks.

At home, I'm barely able to manage the two brown paper sacks while kicking the car door shut, but I take it as another small victory when I do. I can hardly see over the top of the bags as I squeeze them to me and blindly make my way toward the house. I hear the front door open and the load lightens as someone takes the bags from my arms.

"Let me help you there Doris." A deep familiar voice stops me in my tracks.

Carl is there with a half smile. I'm completely frozen in my bewilderment.

"Carl?" I manage to spit it out as a question even though I know it is him.

He brings the groceries up the steps and sets them on the porch. My mother's face disappears from the front window. The kids are yelling inside.

"Oh, my God, I can't believe you're here. When did you get out?" I rush in to hug him, turning my head into his chest.

He hugs me tightly and I take a deep breath. His smell brings in a swirl of emotions and reality from the last time we saw each other. It seems like a lifetime ago.

When I pull back I take him in, he looks handsome but different. His goatee is back, thick and short. He's a little thinner and a lot paler to me but it may just be a lag in my memory. He's wearing a slightly stained white short sleeved shirt untucked and unbuttoned to reveal just a bit of chest hair. His face is relaxed but his eyes hold questions.

He steps back, obviously taking me in too. I self-consciously smooth the scarf on my head and pat at my dark pants in case they are still dusty from the factory. I give him a small smile and wonder if there's any makeup left on my face from this morning. I was so excited about my check that I haven't looked in a mirror for hours.

"I got out Wednesday." He starts abruptly. "A guy I met at the march gathered up some cash and the Judge let me out with a $50 fine and a warning not to return to his county. I hitched back up here over the last few days. I stopped here first, then I'm crashing in Ann Arbor with a couple of guys." His hands are shoved in his pockets and he kicks the grass like a school boy. "If that's alright, you know?"

I'm not sure what he is asking so I just nod. I'm relieved that he's not planning to stay here but also a little rejected. The thoughts and feelings move so quickly through me I settle on being confused and invite him back to the house.

"I know the kids'll be excited to see you. Scott's been asking about you. I just need to change and I'll get supper ready, if my mom hasn't started something."

"Uh, I'll come in and sit with the kids a little longer but then I gotta get going. My ride'll be back around to get me here soon."

Carl puts the groceries on the counter in the kitchen and my mother starts putting them away.

"Go make yourself presentable. I have some hot dogs warming on the stove." She says with a meaningful look.

"He's not staying." I whisper and head to the bedroom.

I decide I'm not going to try too hard to get dolled up since I don't know what to make of the situation. I don't want to look desperate but I don't want to look like I've given up either. I settle on a homemade shift dress that he has seen a hundred times and a little powder on my face. My hair is beyond help after a day in the hot factory so I leave it under the scarf.

Carl's on the floor with Scott in his lap and Suzy is bringing him every block she can find scattered on the floor. He stacks each one she brings, he and Scott count them as the tower gets taller. I lean against the corner and watch the scene.

The tower, in all its attempts at balance and perfection, eventually becomes crooked and too tall, before toppling into Scott's lap. He and Carl clap and cheer but Suzy stands holding another block with a surprised look on her face before she starts to cry.

"Oh, baby girl." I say and pick her up. "It's okay. If you want, we can build it again."

Suzy looks at the block in her hand and throws it to the floor.

My mom pops her head around the corner, "I'm gonna get going. The hot dogs are warm and we picked some green beans so those are ready too. There's enough for everybody?" She says as a question directly to Carl.

He smiles and just then a car honks from the street.

"Oh, man, sorry. Thanks though, that's my ride." He gives Scott a big hug but Scott doesn't want to let go.

"No Daddy! Stay!" He yells dangling from Carl's neck. Carl gives him another bear hug and kisses both of his cheeks.

"I'll be back tomorrow to see you, okay buddy?" He looks at me questioningly and I nod. "Tomorrow is not too far."

Scott isn't letting go so my mom comes in and pulls him off."Stay Daddy!" Carl takes Suzy and kisses her and quickly kisses my cheek.

"I'll call you later. We can talk." He looks from me to Scott and winks. "Sorry," he says and is out the door in a couple strides. Scott continues to cry, "Daddy!" as he and my mom watch Carl leave through the window.

#

(Present)

There's a light knock on the door and it opens before I can get out of my chair to answer it. A friendly looking girl wearing colorful clothing pushes a cart into my room. She begins speaking loudly.

"Hi Doris. I have your morning medicine, okay?"

I clear my throat and speak as loudly as I can. "Okay! What are they for again?"

The girl looks startled and smiles, she hands me a small cup with four pills.

"These are your vitamins," She answers at a regular volume and points to a couple large oval pills. "These ones are for your blood pressure, and these are for your memory," pointing out the two smaller ones.

"What's wrong with my memory?" I ask trying to remember the last time I even saw a doctor.

"You have Alzheimer's, Doris. This pill helps with that." She moves some stuff around on her cart and I sense annoyance in her tone.

The word Alzheimer's doesn't mean anything but I feel like I should know what it is so I try to cover my tracks.

"Oh yeah, this pill helps with that?" I say hoping to get a little more information so maybe I can remember.

"Yup. So the doctor wants you to take these four pills, okay? Are you ready?" Her voice gets louder again which adds annoyance to my worry.

Am I sick? Why don't I remember being at the doctors? Why hasn't anyone talked to me about this before?

I look around the room and notice the hospital bed. Am I in the hospital? What is wrong with me?

The girl holds two small cups in front of me, one with the pills and one with water. Her clothes finally register in my head as scrubs. She must be a nurse.

"Are you a nurse?" I ignore the cups as they hover in front of my face. "You look too young to be a nurse. You look like a teenager."

The girl lets out a breath and puts the cups down. She glances at the clock then sits at the foot of the bed resting her arm on her cart.

"Thank you, Doris. I am a nurse, and I'm 25 years old. So I'm far from being a teenager." She gives another sigh.

I laugh out loud.

"Not as far as me! Twenty-five is still a baby. I think I was around your age when I first started working at the factory. I was the only woman on the line then, and I was married. Carl was gone though…"

An image of Carl flashes through my mind, where was Carl?

"It must have been harder then, being the only woman with all those guys. You were brave Mrs. Doris." The young girl stands again. I don't want her to go.

"None of those fellas knew what to do with me. Half of them didn't want to work with a woman and told me so. Some tried to make it harder for me, some felt like they couldn't let me do things that were my job because they were trying to be polite. But I told them 'just let me do my work the same as you, no more, no less.'"

I paused, leaned forward and lowered my voice, "A fella tried to get fresh with me during a break one time so I had to let him know I wasn't like that. I kicked him, where it counts, and another guy came by and grabbed him. It was a crazy time then…" The fear of that day trickles in and I lose track of my story..

"It sounds like it, Mrs. Doris, that's too bad." She holds up the two small paper cups again, one with the medicine and one with the water. "I've got to get on to the next room though. How about you take your pills and we can finish our chat later?"

"What are these for?" I ask tipping the cup and watching

the pills slide back and forth. Two big ones and two little ones.

The nurse takes in a breath. "They'll keep you healthy," she answers a little short. Then she takes the cup back, flips my hand over and dumps two small pills into my palm.

"There, now put those in your mouth then take a drink, okay?"

I shrug and do what she says, the pills scratch a little as they go down my throat. Again, she takes my hand and dumps the two large pills out into it.

"Do the same with those, put them in your mouth, then drink the rest of your water." She taps the hand with the pills in it and I move it to my mouth to put them in. She taps the water cup and I drink that in turn.

The large pills feel hard in my throat and I cough a little. "Take some more water Doris, I will leave this one here in case you need it. She puts a large Styrofoam cup with a lid and a straw on the small table near my recliner, then backs her cart out of the room with a wave.

I slide into my chair and cough a little more. I try to swallow hard and I feel like I have a lump in my throat. I cough again and wish I had some water or coffee. I do a couple more hard swallows and the lump feels like it is moving down. I make a mental note to get some water the next time I am up.

#

Past (October 1963)

The kids are asleep and it is the first time Carl and I have been alone together since he came back two days ago. I'm exhausted but I know we have to talk. I still don't know what to say.

He apparently doesn't either because the silence stretches on while he uses a toothpick to scrape food remnants from the edge of the kitchen table.

"Coffee?" I ask as I pour the last from the percolator into a mug.

Carl takes it and swirls the lukewarm liquid with his finger. "Thanks."

Silence.

"Okay, I know we need to talk but I don't know what to talk about first." I sit down across from him, my hands are shaking.

"I don't really either." He says looking at his coffee.

More silence. I can't take it.

"Well, what do you want Carl? You are the one who left, can you at least tell me what you want?"

I'm trying to push down the feelings of annoyance. I just want him to take the lead, be the man, tell me what to do. I don't have the energy, I am so tired.

The last couple days I've debated what I want. I feel like I might not need Carl, like I could do this on my own. This is the first time being on my own is an option, even if it is a controversial one. I like working. I like knowing that we are taken care of and feeling in control of what is happening in my life.

If Carl comes back will I have to quit? He doesn't have a job. I don't know if I can go back to sitting at home with the kids and pretending. I definitely don't want to listen to him complain about a job he hates anymore either.

"Do you love me?" Carl looks directly into my eyes.

His eyes are intense, like they used to be when we would hang out at the coffee shop and talk about the world and life.

Typical of Carl to start with the hardest question first, the question I never factored in.

I don't trust myself to know the answer to this one.

Need and love have been so tightly wrapped together my whole life that I'm not sure how to separate the two. If I don't *need* Carl, is there love left? When I imagine my life without him there is fear of drowning in failure. When I imagine my life with him there is fear of suffocating in expectation.

Either way, I can't breathe.

Carl gets up and moves to the chair next to me. He grabs my hands and kisses them. "You have to tell me if you really love me, it makes all the difference."

His eyes shine with tears. I think back to when we were dating.

What I loved about Carl was the freedom he offered. I thought it was freedom to leave here but really it was freedom to find my own thoughts and decide who I would be. Carl didn't come with expectations. I put those on us, and on him. He has always just wanted me to be happy, maybe we can be.

"I do love you," it's hard to speak above a whisper. "I'm just afraid."

I take my hands back to cover my face, I try to muffle the sobs with the seam of my dress.

Carl is quiet, he scoots his chair closer so our knees are touching. He leans down and kisses the top of my head. I hear his breath shudder, he puts his head in his hands. I hear him start to cry. Our legs and heads are touching, like an almost embrace, and we cry together until we are both out of tears.

He gives me his handkerchief and I self-consciously try to clean the tears from my hands and face. He's also tear streaked and red.

I hand him back the handkerchief, he wipes his face then gives me a sly grin and blows his nose, long and loud, like a goose call.

"Carl!" I'm startled, I can't help but smile, the uncomfortable tension is broken with his chuckle.

"Doris, I love you too. Let's just leave it at that tonight. Love is a good place to start." He pulls me in and kisses me on the lips for the first time in a month.

I return the kiss fully, with my heart wide open for the first time since the kids were born, maybe even longer.

We hold each other and kiss for a while before Carl gets up to go.

I consider asking him to stay but before I can ask, he answers. "This was good Doris, I've gotta go. Thank you."

He leans down and brushes his lips across mine one last time. "See you tomorrow, love."

I watch him get into the rusted Caprice he's been borrowing from his friend and pull away.

My heart feels light and happy but my mind has already started racing. We still have so much to figure out.

#

(Present)

It's nice to have someone in my bed again, even if it is just for a while. I can feel the warmth from where he lay just a moment ago.

Now he kneels next to the bed, his face level with mine. He kisses my forehead and raises to go. I reach out and let my fingers trail down the sleeve of his black shirt to his hand and I squeeze. He looks at me for a moment then winks. He shuffles toward the doorway and disappears.

I roll over toward the wall and fall asleep.

\#

"Doris! You can't sleep in here!" A tall skinny woman shakes my foot as it's suspended in the air off the end of the bed.

"This isn't your bed, let me help you up." She walks to the side of the bed, I roll to my back, but I am at the edge of the bed and start to fall.

"Whoa, be careful!" I feel the woman's knee under my bottom and try to find the floor with my foot to push myself back up.

"Okay, Doris, take it easy." She guides my leg from the bed to the floor. I grip the sheets with my hands to keep from sliding.

With both feet on the floor I stop sliding and get my bearings. She helps me to scoot my whole behind back on the bed.

"Are you alright?" She asks with relief in her voice. "That was close. What're you doing in here?"

I look around the room. Nothing looks familiar. I rub my face before I answer her. "Sleeping?"

She chuckles, "Well, where's your walker?"

I stare blankly at her, this does not ring a bell.

"You need to be using the walker Doris, you could have a fall. Can you stay here a minute while I get someone to help find it?" I look at the woman's name tag and it reads Faye.

I nod and she leaves the room. I lay back on the bed. Why do I feel so tired?

It seems an instant later she's back and tapping my leg. She's brought both a walker and some assistance.

"This is Eva, and we're going to help you get back to your room, okay Doris?"

"I used to have a girl named Faye who watched my kids when they were little." I say to her as she wraps a thick plastic belt around my waist.

"How nice." She pulls the belt tight so my skin bulges over the top of it. I must have made a face because she adds, "It will loosen once you stand up, don't worry."

Faye gives me a pursed lip smile, she and Eva count to three then yank up on the belt.

My bottom hops up off the bed then plunks quickly back down.

"You're going to have to help a little Doris, we need you to stand up."

"I can do that." Without waiting, I start to push up from the bed and the girls grip the belt and pull. "See?" I say with satisfaction once I am standing.

Faye puts my hands on the grips of the walker. "Try to keep your walker with you Doris, for when you're feeling weak. Pretend it's your dance partner, you never want to abandon your dance partner, right?"

"I suppose not." I say, but I don't understand what she means. The three of us leave the room and head down a long wide hallway.

"Here is your place, Doris." Faye points to a wide wooden door decorated with a wreath of photos and white plastic carnations. A sign to the left of the door says Doris Atkins.

"I guess so." I say and I push my walker inside.

Faye follows me but the other girl disappears down the hallway.

"Let me get you settled in." Faye moves a blanket and

a stuffed rabbit from a reclining chair, "How about you sit here and I'll come back for you at dinnertime."

I move the walker aside and take a few steps to the recliner while Faye checks something on her phone. After I sit in the chair, she puts the blanket in my lap and turns on the TV. "Will this channel be alright?" There are a few men riding horses and shooting each other in technicolor racing around the screen.

"I guess so."

Faye pats my hair and says she'll be back later. On her way to the door, she pushes the walker out of her way against the end of the bed.

#

13

(October 1963)

Scott is up early and excited because today is his birthday. He crawls into bed with me and pats my hair and cheeks until I open my eyes. I leave them shut longer than I need to because I love how small and gentle his hands are and I know he'll stop when I open my eyes.

"Mommy….mommy…" He whispers loudly just inches from my nose, his warm breath tickles.

I can't help but smile and squeeze him tight while we both giggle.

"Mommy! Get up!" He's bouncing on his knees all over the bed now, I'm just trying not to get kicked.

"No, I'm too tired." I say and pull the blanket up over my head and pretend to snore.

"Moooommmy!" Scott tugs on the blankets, "You have to make my cake today!"

"What? Why would I do that?" I peek over the blanket at him as his eyes get huge.

He yells as loud as he can. "IT"S MY BIRTHDAY!! And you said I get cake!"

"Oh, that's right, you are having a birthday." I grab him again and kiss his face. "I suppose I better get up then."

The mornings are cold even early in October this year, I grab my heavy robe and an old pair of Carl's socks to layer over my pajamas before I shuffle to the kitchen.

I start the percolator and make Scott a bowl of Co-Co Wheats before Suzy starts making sounds. I check the clock, it's not even 7 a.m. So much for sleeping in on my day off.

Once everyone is fed and washed up Scott starts in about his birthday again, "When is Dad coming over. Is he coming soon? When is Grandma coming? Can I see my present?"

He's pretty relentless for the next two hours. Finally, I give in and call my Mother to come over to take the kids outside while I start on the cake.

It's warmed up to be a beautiful sunny Autumn day. I've invited my mother and brother over for lunch and cake to celebrate.

A small package arrived yesterday for Scott from Carl's mother which I told him he had to save until today. With everything going on I decided to try, for today, to let myself relax and not think too much. I want today to be about Scott and family.

The kids and my mom are still outside when I take the cakes from the oven to cool. I'm planning to attempt my first ever layer cake.

The only Woman's Day magazine in the factory breakroom has convinced me that it's so easy, even I can do it. Of course, I have almost memorized the magazine because it's the only one available there that isn't full of suggestive looking ladies leaning on cars or political stories that get the guys riled up and red in the face.

When the trio come in, I let the kids help make the frosting. I purchased it as a mix because the magazine ads highly recommended it and I've never made frosting.

My mother regards this as laziness on my part and mutters about "young people and their shortcuts" while she starts on the dishes. She's then doubly appalled when I let each child run into the living room to watch cartoons while licking a frosting coated mixing spoon.

"Doris, are you sure you don't want me to help with the cake? I brought my icing spatula, which should be able to smooth out that mix frosting you have."

"I've got it mother." I respond with forced politeness. I want to do this cake right and on my own.

The magazine made it seem like any woman could do it easily and that every family wants a mother who can make this cake. When I asked my mother two weeks ago if I could borrow her cake stand she insisted that I should just let her make the cake. Maybe it's because my mother has been so convinced that I couldn't make it, that I'm obsessing about it.

When Carl arrives he's attacked by two chocolate covered monsters. The frosting around their mouth has dribbled down their chins forming a sort-of mock goatee.

"You kids look just like your Daddy with that chocolate on your chins!" I tell them and this makes Scott laugh. Soon he's wearing Carl's shoes and talking in a deep voice repeating "I'm Daddy, call me Carl."

"Is that what I look like?" Carl asks as he kisses my cheek.

"Exactly." I reply with a smirk. He tries to kiss me again but I slap him away. My mother huffs at both of us before she drags the kids to the bathroom to get washed up for lunch.

When David arrives, he and Carl immediately begin discussing the happenings of the civil rights movement and I know that I have lost Carl's attention until I pry them apart to eat. I'm glad David and Carl get along so well, it sort of evens out the dynamics since my father is rarely around.

I'm still pondering my family as I begin to remove the cooled cakes from their well floured pans. The first two come out easily. I trim the tops, and set one on the milky white glass cake stand. I carefully stack the second golden cake on top of the thick layer of fudge frosting I've spread on the first, being mindful to line them up just right.

I feel pretty good as I gently tap the bottom of the third pan of soft yellow cake. I give it a little shake and slowly lift the pan to peek under. I see the cake resting on the counter. This gives me confidence and I lift the pan the rest of the way up with more gusto than I intend. When I look down at the counter I see that only three quarters of my precious cake has made it out, the last jagged quarter is still firmly set in the pan.

"Shit!" I mutter to myself, and hear my mother coming into the kitchen.

"Doris can I help with anything?"

I slam the pan back over the torn layer before she can see, "Sure, can you take the sandwiches and chips? I'll bring out the drinks." I say with a fake smile.

I hand her the tray before she gets to the counter. I put the cups and pitcher of Kool-Aid on the table then rush back to the kitchen. I don't want to give her the chance to poke around.

"Mom, I'm just finishing up the layers on the cake. Can you make sure the kids don't get in here, I need to concentrate."

"Sure honey, I don't know what there is to concentrate on with a birthday cake, but I'll keep the kids out here." She chuckles condescendingly.

Back at the counter, I lift up the pan slowly, half hoping it has somehow melded together, but it only appears worse. When I slammed the pan down, I smashed the part of the cake that was out of the pan before and managed to break the part that was stuck in the pan into pieces.

Ugh.

I look at the two beautiful layers I have already put to-gether, a twinge of hope sparks an idea. Maybe if I take them apart I can put the broken one in between and it won't be notice-able.

Initially, this plan seems brilliant. I optimistically begin by using the spatula my mother brought and a slight twisting motion to pull the top layer of cake from the bottom.

I try to steady it by carefully securing the cake with my hand on the unfrosted side. Unfortunately, the frosting from the bottom cake has created some sort of suction and the middle pulls almost completely from the top layer of the cake.

I let out a silent scream as the layer I'm holding then folds into itself crumbling into pieces. In a moment of complete frus-tration I throw the spatula down and manage to gash the side of my last remaining intact cake layer.

"Crap, shit!" I half whisper as I mime stomping the length of the kitchen.

I take a step back and look at the counter. The image of the cake from the magazine dances mockingly in my head while I stare in bewilderment at my disaster. How did I manage this? It's as if a cake bomb went off on my counter.

Again, the magazine images come to mind. I can see the smiling woman standing proudly next to the beautiful layer cake. She has perfectly coiffed hair and not a spot on her white apron.

I look down at my hands and shirt, both smeared in frost-ing and yellow cake bits. I think of my children covered in frost-ing from licking the spoons earlier and how I must look simi-larly ridiculous. From somewhere deep inside a giggle starts, I cannot help but laugh at the incredible mess I am. I laugh so hard tears well up and squeeze from the corners of my eyes.

The laughing won't stop, it pushes itself out until my ribs ache, it feels soul cleansing. I look at the cake again and try to regain my composure before someone hears me.

"Now what am I going to do?" I ask myself. My eyes settle on the deep, clear glass cover of the cake stand. It has a flat top where a flower shaped knob was once attached, it broke off and was lost long ago.

I flip it over and inspect it as an idea forms in my head. I spoon a couple globs of frosting from the mixing bowl and smear them around in the bottom of the lid. I grab handfuls of cake and tear it into large spongy pieces dumping them onto the frosting. I continue to layer the cake bits and frosting until the lid is almost full.

"Hey, you about done Doris?" Carl pops his head into the kitchen and startles me.

"Oh, God Carl, you scared the Jesus out of me. What do you think?" I hold out my creation to him like a child showing off a mud pie.

"Whoa? Is it supposed to look like that?" He asks with trepidation, then adds encouragingly, "My mom's trifles looked sort of like that."

"Um, yeah, it's a new thing. It's a cake but layered like a trifle." I put it back on the counter, shake some sprinkles on and pop in some birthday candles. "Yup. It's definitely supposed to look like this." I whisper.

I clear my throat and carry my creation to the living room yelling cheerfully. "Who's ready for dessert! Let's light the candles and sing to the Birthday Boy!"

#

(Present)

"We are going to a party?" I ask as I pat my hair in the mirror. There seems to be a large piece in the back that wants to stick up and I can't get it to stay down.

"Yes, mom, it's a birthday party for Scott." Suzy says as she steers me away from the mirror. "And stop touching your hair, the hairdresser here got the bun in it beautifully and if you keep poking it you'll wreck it."

I can't help but reach up toward my hair to touch the thin bundle on top of my head.   "How old is Scott?" I ask racking my brain for a mental image.

"Mom! Stop! Seriously, it's fine" Suzy pushes my hand away from my hair. "Scott is turning 59 tomorrow. We're going to Haab's tonight since Scott's in town and we thought you might enjoy the old place. We don't want to be late, I'll get you a sweater so we can go."

Scott is in town? I think to myself, trying to figure out what she means. Where does Scott live? I'm trying to decide if I should ask but I notice Suzy getting into the closet. She takes out two sweaters.

One is light blue with a collar and has fuzzy looking hairs all over, it looks stuffy and uncomfortable. The other is navy blue with pearl buttons and a thin smooth knit.

Suzy seems to be debating between the two. She apparently comes to a decision because she hangs the navy sweater on a hook in the closet and holds the fuzzy sweater out for me to put on.

I don't like that sweater I think to myself. I stare at the sweater and try to figure out what to do. I'm searching for words. I don't want to wear it but Suzy is shaking it at me insistently. I take a step back.

"It's fuzzy." I tell her even though that's not exactly what I want to say.

"Yes, and thick. It will keep you warm until we get there, now please take it." She shakes it at me again.

"Fuzzy." I repeat but she ignores me and shoves it into my hand impatiently.

My hand squeezes into the thick fuzzy bundle and the sensation takes my breath away. I drop the sweater and look at Suzy, then at the closet. I can see the navy sweater hanging on the hook. I walk toward the closet.

"Mom, come on. Let me help you with the sweater, then we can go. Okay?" Suzy picks up the sweater from the floor and steps in front of me just before I can get to the closet.

She holds it open it in with two hands. "Just put your left arm in first Mom." She smiles, "I can help you from there."

I know I don't want to wear this sweater so I shake my head no, and try to find the words.

Suzy groans, I can see she is frustrated. "Mom, it's too cold for you to go out in bare arms." She touches the short sleeve of my white and navy polka dot shirt. "Please put on your sweater."

I lift my arm and start to glide it into the sleeve but it's thickness and the pokey hairs remind me that I do not want to wear this sweater.

I pull my arm out quickly and manage to spit out the word "itchy."

Suzy pets the sweater and looks at me with furrowed brows. "Mom," She asks thoughtfully, "do you *want* to wear this sweater?"

I shake my head no. Suzy takes another deep breath, but this time she looks a little sad.

"I'm sorry. I should have asked, I just never know where

you'll be at." She leans in and kisses my cheek.

She hangs the fuzzy sweater back on the hook and picks up the navy one. "Would you like to wear this sweater?"

"That'll do." I say with a smile and she helps me into the sweater.

#

(Fall 1963)

"You know this is silly, Doris." My mother says as she hands me the dress she just finished ironing.

"You two are married, why are you calling this a date and when is he going to move back in! No one in town knows what to make of you two."

It's been weeks now since Carl and I decided to move slowly. Carl is still hurt about Paul and I'm still worried about feeling suffocated. We both love each other and thought it would be best to let our minds settle and our hearts heal before we jump back into "normal" life.

"I know you don't understand but this is about me and Carl, and neither of us care what anyone else 'makes' of us." I say from the bathroom as I get changed from my work clothes.

"But why live separately, you're married? Are you considering a.." Her voice drops to a whisper and she peeks her head into the bathroom, "divorce?"

"Not right now, but I guess it's an option. Carl is still upset and we don't want to hurt each other more. This is just what's going to work for us right now." I realize I might as well be speaking Greek to my mother because if it's not practical, she's not going to understand it.

"You kids are so casual with your families, what about

these babies? What will people say to them when they get to school? Don't you want them to have a respectable family?"

Now my mother is picking at a spot she knows will get to me, but I'm not going to get sucked in. I consider bringing up my own "respectable" childhood but it's not worth hurting her.

"Mom, we have a little time before we have to worry about the kids social status. AND only you *old* people get worked up about that stuff anymore, so please, just give it a break." I half smile to myself because I know she hates to think of herself as old.

"I'm not old! And if being young means running around without respectable values and only worrying about being 'happy' and all your 'feelings' all the time then maybe I *am* old! Doris, you're gonna make me need a cigarette." She pats her skirt pocket and heads out to the back porch.

I roll my eyes at her and add some eyeliner out past the corner of my eye, a-la Audrey Hepburn. There's a knock at the door and the kids yell "Daddy!"

"Anyone home!" Carl shouts from the front door.

I come out and do a little twirl in my reworked house-dress. I've added a loose belt and shortened the hemline a bit to make it more modern. Carl and Scott clap at my entrance. I hug and kiss the kids and yell out to my Mother that we're leaving.

She comes in to wag her finger at us.

"Don't go getting into trouble and don't stay out too late. This young lady has to work tomorrow." She gives Carl a look that is meant to make him feel guilty about my working.

"Mom, stop. We'll be at the theater in Ann Arbor watching that *Lillies of the Field* movie, then dinner, then home." I grab Carl's hand, he gives her a salute before we get out the door.

"So she's still not real pleased with us?" Carl asks jokingly when we get in the car.

"We just aren't doing what we're supposed to do I guess." I realize that I'm in the driver's seat, out of habit.

"Did you want to drive?" I shake the keys at him.

"I don't need to drive, you know where we're going." Carl lights up a cigarette.

We head south a few blocks, when we stop at the corner light. I look hard at Carl. He's slouched down in the seat drumming his fingers on the edge of the window.

"Penny for your thoughts?" He says playfully.

I feel like I'm about to give him more than a penny's worth. I've made a decision.

"I don't want to quit work, I like it. I'm afraid I'll have to quit if you move back in."

Carl looks a little surprised and takes a drag off his cigarette before he flicks it out the window.

"Alright," he says slowly as the smoke rolls from his mouth. "If we're being straight, I don't want to go back to work, I want to sculpt and stay home with the kids."

A car behind me honks. I drive to the next block and pull over.

"You want to stay home?" I put the car in park. I had never considered this. When I considered telling Carl that I wanted to work, I thought we may agree that I work part time and he would find a job he liked better than factory work somewhere. It had not occurred to me that I might bring the only steady income.

"Yes," Carl replies emphatically. "I kept thinking about my life while I was in jail, I kept thinking about us. I realized how we turned into the people I never wanted to be."

Carl touches my cheek. "It kills me, you know, about Paul..." He swallows hard.

"But I wasn't even being me, I was just doing the thing that I thought you wanted. So I can see how you might have wanted to be with someone real…"

A few tears escape his eyes and race to his chin. "So you didn't really go out on me, not the real me. And I never even asked who you wanted to be, so maybe that wasn't the real you." He wipes his face with the back of his sleeve before he continues.

"If we are going to do this, I want it to be you and me being us, finding our own way. I don't care about other people. I want our kids to see they have brave parents. Are we brave enough to be happy?"

He grabs my hand and kisses the back of it.

"Doris, can you be happy with *me*?"

I'm terrified and relieved at the same time. To my heart, and my seldom acknowledged soul, his words are everything real and true.

But my thoughts race ahead to shake me.

The voices of reality and propriety swirl together in my head. "This isn't how women behave." "This sounds great but it's impossible. It's too hard." "This town won't let you do it. You'll never be normal." "What about your kids?" "Your mother is right."

I stare out the window where the brown fallen leaves have gathered on the sidewalk.

A pair of girls walk through the pile, crushing the dry leaves with each step. The girls talk loudly and swing their loose straight hair over their shoulders. Both wear stiff, bright colored skirts that stop inches above their knees and long jackets with bits of fur on them as protection from the autumn air. They look so young and modern. The thought makes me smile. Maybe change is coming, maybe even here in this little town.

#

(Present)

Brown leaves scurry across the sidewalk in front of two women as they walk arm in arm around the circle path. They each wear a puffy jacket but I imagine they are still cold. I press my hand against the window and its chill passes through me.

The shiver brings the sensation of pressure to my abdomen. I feel a twinge of anxiety. My groin and stomach tighten to balance the pressure.

I walk over to the open doorway and poke my head out. I see a few people at the end of the hall chatting. The faint sound of Beatles music comes from the other direction. Carl loved the Beatles. I step out to follow the music.

After a few steps the pressure is back with more urgency this time. I feel antsy and start to walk faster. Somewhere in my mind I recognize the sensation and know there is something I need to do. I start to sweat. What am I going to do?

"Doris?" A woman's voice calls from behind me, "Can I help you with something?" She looks concerned and walks briskly to catch up with me.

"Yessss…" I say dragging the word out as I try to put my problem into words.

Suddenly, the pressure releases and warmth spreads between my legs. I look down instinctively but see only my tan slacks and slippers. I'm unsure of what just happened so I look at the woman standing before me.

She looks back at me with expectation. "Doris? Are you alright?"

I have a sense of relief as I contemplate the woman's question. "Yes, yes, alright." I say nodding. The woman looks unsure, I wonder if I gave her the wrong answer. I search my mind again for the question.

"Okay, well, I'm working your hall tonight. Do you remember me? I'm Faye" She taps her name badge to show me. The black letters stand out from the gold but mean nothing in the quick glimpse I get.

"Do you want to come down for the Celebrity Name Game in the lounge? We're doing Oscar winners from 1965 to 1975!" Her voice has more enthusiasm than her face.

She guides me toward a small group of people standing at the end of the hall. We pass a couple doors before she stops abruptly and asks, "Would you like to use the restroom before we get down there?"

I nod so she guides me back into my room.

"Let's take your walker with us when we head back out, okay Doris?" She taps the green handle on the walker as we walk past it to the bathroom.

At the toilet I start to tug at my pants and underwear. My pants slip down but I have a hard time gripping the thin web-like material of the strange looking underwear.

"When did you start wearing Depends?" Faye asks and steps back into the room.

I'm not sure I understand the question so I continue to pull down on the snug fitting sides of the briefs.

Faye appears in the bathroom again with a clipboard and she releases a groan.

"This is not your protocol for beginning an incontinence program."

Her eyes dart around the room and rest on a plastic package on the shower stool. She walks over and grabs it, "These aren't even the right size for you, these are too small. Where did they get these?"

She tosses the package back onto the bed in the other room.

"Here, sorry Doris, let me help you." She reaches over and tears the side webbing of the brief so it slips down easily. "It looks like you made good use of them though."

"I'll talk to someone and figure this out." She checks her watch then pulls a cord hanging next to the toilet. A red light and a voice from a small speaker answer quickly, "Can we help you Miss Atkins?"

"This is Faye, I have Doris in the restroom here, she needs her aide to help her finish up and get her down to the lounge. I need to get to my rounds. Please remind them she NEEDS to have her walker."

"She'll be down in a minute." The speaker responds and the light goes off.

"Why don't you have a seat here, try to use the restroom, your aide will be here in a sec. Wait here for her, she'll help you with your underwear."

"So you'll wait, right?" She looks at me intensely so I nod.

Faye disappears and I'm left on the loo staring at the swollen undergarment hanging on just one leg. I notice the left side is torn so I pull at the right side and it starts to tear. I manage to pull it off and look for the trash.

I see one near the door so I try to toss the bundle in. It misses and I watch it slide just outside the doorway into the next room.

I need to go pick it up.

I struggle to get my pants up to my hips. My hands don't

seem to want to hold the waistband. I can see the edge of the brief still peeking around the doorjamb at me.

I waddle over to retrieve it. I feel unsteady with my slacks sagging from my hips and dragging under my heels. I hold the wall and try to squat to reach the brief.

Only, when I crouch down it is further away than I thought and I have to lean through the doorway to get it. I finally reach it and am able to tug it closer to me with just two fingers.

As I stand triumphantly with my prize, I lose my grip on the wall and fall forward into the edge of the open door.

Pain shoots through my head and shoulder, my face finds the rough looped carpet and warmth spreads across my cheek. I'm stunned, motionless. Other than the burning in my face, no individual part of my body is registering. I feel like a heap on the floor. I can't figure out how to begin to move.

"Oh, shit!" I hear shouting from above. "We're gonna need help in here!"

"Doris, what happened? Are you okay? Oh, my God." I'm rolled slowly onto my back and a young round faced blonde comes into focus. I attempt a smile and reach up but she holds me back with a gentle hand.

"Wait here, it's okay, we'll get you cleaned up." Her voice is calm but her face looks worried. " Let me fix your pants."

I feel a tugging on my pants then a number of other people are buzzing around the room. The activity and my throbbing head makes me tired.

Pain shoots through my shoulder and chest now. I try again to move my arm but it feels like lead. I give up, it is easier to just close my eyes.

#

14

"Oh my God! Carl is it true?" I say as soon as I'm home. "It can't be true. Oh, my God."

Carl is sitting on the floor just a couple feet from the television, his face is wet with tears. The black and white images of somber television anchors and pictures of the president flash across the screen. My mother sits on the couch rocking a reluctant Suzy and muttering prayers.

"Doris, they killed him. He was making changes." Carl says with a mixture of frustration and despair. "Now what are we going to do?"

The thought that someone would kill our president was horrifying. Especially out in front of all those people. I can't help but get teary eyed as well. I know that Carl will take this personally, he really believed in President Kennedy and what he could do to help the country.

"I'm so sorry, Carl." I sit down next to him and hug him close.

"Mommy!" Scott comes running into the living room and wraps his arms around my neck. "Mommy, did you see that a bad guy shot Kennedy?"

Scott has a plastic pistol tucked into his pocket, he pulls it out and aims it each person in the room. "Pew, pew, pew, pew."

"That's enough!" Carl snatches the gun from Scotts and storms off to the bedroom.

Scott looks at me with wide eyes. I kneel down and hold his hands.

"Scotty, when people get shot they die, and it makes people sad when other people die. Daddy, Mommy and Grandma are sad because President Kennedy died.

So right now, we don't want to think about guns or shooting people, okay?" Scott nods his head and comes in for a hug. "Why don't you see if one of the other boys wants to play outside. Wear your mittens, it's cold."

He runs off to the back door to get his coat and boots. I get up and take Suzy from my mother.

"What is this world coming to? He was so young... Poor Jackie." My mother says shaking her head. "She has those children all on her own now."

"Women are strong when they need to be mom. She'll be alright." I give my mom a peck on the cheek.

I lay Suzy in her crib for a nap then go into the kitchen. The sink is full and I don't think I've ever been more relieved to see dirty dishes. Today they give me something to do with my hands while the world ponders Kennedy's death. They are a physical anchor to this house and the safety of my own family.

I fill the sink with warm water and swish my hand around to make foamy bubbles on the water's surface. I pick at dried oatmeal bits in bowls and scrub at coffee rings on cups.

For each fork and spoon I wash I say a prayer of thanks for the safety of the mouth that used it. I add a prayer of strength for poor Mrs. Kennedy.

#

(Present)

"Can you squeeze the wash cloth Mrs. Atkins?" An eager young girl in a red polo shirt prompts encouragingly.

Sitting on the edge of the bed in a small curtained room, I try to follow her instructions. The young lady has a small pink tub half full of soapy water sitting on a tray table in front of me, there's a damp washcloth held loosely the hand resting in my lap.

I stare at the young lady then back to the washcloth.

"Mrs. Atkins, we are getting you washed up for the day. Can you squeeze the washcloth and wipe your face?"

I hear the words the girl is saying but can't get the meaning out of them. I know she wants me to do something.

"Let me help you, okay?" She rolls her stool in closer and holds my elbow in one hand while her other hand helps me grip the washcloth. She starts to lift my hand toward my face.

Suddenly my body knows what to do and my hand clenches the cloth. I bring up my arm without her support.

"Good, Mrs. Atkins. Wash your face."

I find my cheek with the cloth and start to rub, I feel cool drips of water running down my arm and falling onto my lap.

"Now can you move it around and wash your whole face?" The young lady is miming rubbing the cloth in a circle over her face. I look at my arm as it moves up and down in the air.

The girl continues to move her hand around her face, I stretch out my arm towards her in an attempt to match her

182

movements. I know this isn't exactly right. She ducks out of the way and giggles.

"No, Mrs. Atkins, we are washing YOUR face. Let me help you."

I smile at the girl, we are having fun.

She bends my arm and holds my hand. She gently glides my hand and the cloth in a circle around the edge of my face. The rough cloth spreads it's cool water on my cheek and over my forehead.

"Good, good. Now let me finish this up for you, and we can get you dressed." She dips the cloth back in the water and rings it out before rubbing it with careful, efficient strokes over my face and neck.

"Is that better?" she asks with a smile.

I touch the tingly dampness on my cheek and smile back. Yes, I think to myself, but the word doesn't come out.

#

(May 1964)

My mom gives me a long hug and a kiss on the cheek before she leaves. As she pulls away from the curb in the early morning light, I don't know how to feel.

"They found your father in an apartment in Detroit this morning." She'd said, her voice struggling for control. "He apparently passed out in a friend's bathroom. They think he fell and hit his head. Your brother and I are going to go see him. The doctor said it's pretty bad."

I told her I would be there later, that I needed to figure things out here first.

She looked upset that I wasn't going with her and David now, but I just couldn't leave. I need some time.

No one has heard from or seen my father in months.

I think we all assumed he wasn't coming back but the uncertainty of not knowing where he was had somehow given me a cushion of time so it wasn't reality yet. I don't know that anyone hoped he would come back, we knew that when he was home he was a burden. His absence meant no one had to be responsible for him, we could all just pretend he was "away" and leave it at that.

Of course I love him, he is my father, but he's also terribly disappointing.

I wonder if I can be sympathetic when I see him. His lack of responsibility and control over our whole lifetime just angers me. What if I see him, on his deathbed, and I'm still angry? What if I think he deserves it? What kind of person does that make me? What if he asks me to forgive him, a dying man's wish, and I can't do it?

I'm not ready to face all of this.

I resent him more for making me.

I crawl back in bed with Carl.

"Hey babe, what's going on? Aren't you going to work?" he asks as he sleepily kisses my forehead.

"I don't think so." I whisper and start to cry.

He sits up against the pillow and pulls my head to his bare chest. "Oh, babe, it's okay, it's okay." He repeats as he pets my hair. I cry until I can't anymore and he doesn't ask why. He just holds me and tells me it's okay.

It's all I need right now, until I can decide what okay means.

We lay like this until Scott comes and pushes the door

open. "Can I watch T.V?" he says sleepily.

"Sure baby." I go to get out of bed but Carl kisses my head and motions for me to stay.

"I gotcha boy, let's see what's on."

"Captain Kangaroo, Captain Kangaroo!" chants Scott following Carl down the hallway.

I pull a pillow over my face, I'm not sure if I can do this.

I call into work, and get dressed.

I give Carl the little info I have about my father, kiss them all goodbye and head outside into the damp cool wind. I can smell rain in the air and I realize how late spring is arriving this year.

#

(Present)

The brown liquid escapes from its place in the white pile. I push it back with my spoon but it keeps coming, running up to the edges of the green plate.

The spoon makes a scraping noise as I move it back and forth through the brown liquid. I know it will not stop but I try anyway. I feel like it needs to be inside the white pile.

Scrape, scrape, scrape, scrape. Push, push, push, push.

It won't stop. It won't stop. It won't stop.

"It won't stop." I hear myself say.

The sound of my own voice startles me. I look around and see a few other tables with people at them. Across from me sits a man with large eyebrows, he's wearing a black sweatshirt.

"No." he says, "It doesn't stop."

He is so familiar.

"It doesn't stop." I repeat after him and drop my spoon.

"Mrs. Atkins, do you need some help?" A fat woman in a hair net kneels next to me.

"It doesn't stop." I say quietly.

The woman purses her lips causing them to disappear, leaving only her round dimpled cheeks to hold the sympathetic look.

"Why don't you at least finish your shake, honey. It has the stuff to keep you healthy." she says holding up a styrofoam cup with a straw.

"Ha!" the man across the table from me bursts into laughter before he gets up from the table. "Too late!" He calls.

I watch him go. The hair netted woman doesn't seem to notice.

"Right here, Doris." She says and brings the cup into my view. I take it in my hand.

She groans loudly as she gets up. "These old knees aren't holding up." She pushes my hand toward my mouth until the straw from the cup pokes my lips.

"Drink up." She chirps.

I obey and take a long sip of the sweet, milky liquid. Drink up, I think to myself. It echoes in my head, drink up.

#

(June 1964)

"He's on fluid restrictions right now, so if he asks for a drink you can't give him one. A nurse will be by later and give him what he can have." A grey haired doctor warns me before I enter the hospital room.

Just inside the door to my father's room and I freeze, startled by the bags and tubes connected to him. I take a few steps forward.

My father is small, shrunken. His skin is dark and dirty looking. He's facing away from me towards the wall, the back of his hospital gown is open, revealing protruding ribs and shoulder blades. Why is he so skinny?

Dark marks, and trails of veins run over his back and down his arms. His head is bandaged and the grey hair that peeks from under the wrapping is crusted with blood. You can tell he's not well taken care of. A rash of guilt creeps across my chest.

On the drive to the hospital I ran through this encounter in my mind and had it all planned out. He was going to look at me and smile. I wouldn't smile back but would take his hand. He would nod knowingly. He would thank me for being there. I would tell him I love him. Maybe we would hug.

I would leave with him knowing I loved him but getting to keep my anger.

He would keep all the responsibility. I was a good daughter, this was all his fault. We would part with that agreement, nothing more would be needed.

But this is so different. Will he respond if I talk to him? I couldn't possibly touch him.

His body shudders and I hear him exhale loudly.

"Dad?" I somehow manage an audible word.

His head turns slightly, he pulls the sheet up over his shoulder with a shaky hand. Did he hear me?

"Dad, it's me, Doris." I say a little louder and force myself to step up to the edge of his bed.

This time he rolls slowly to his back and looks at me from one swollen eye. He doesn't smile. He just stares.

Neither of us make a sound. We are both just staring.

He points just past me with an unsteady finger. I turn and see a large white bowl on the table. I pick it up and look back at him. He nods weakly and taps the bed next to him. I set the porcelain coated bowl where he tapped.

He rolls himself over the bowl and starts retching foul yellow-pinkish liquid with such force it sloshes over the edge and onto the sheets. I back out of the room and call to a nurse in the hall.

"My father is throwing up everywhere!" I say to her.

She looks at me without alarm. "Yeah, he's going to do that. It's the alcohol withdrawal and his liver's not good. Give me a minute and I'll come in and get him cleaned up." She pushes her cart into the room across the hall.

I'm not sure I can go back in. I sit on a green plastic chair and hold my stomach. The smell is still in my nose, I take deep breaths rocking myself a little.

"You alright sweetie?" The nurse has come back with her cart. "How about you stay here and I'll let you know when he's all set." She gives me a nod and heads into the room, leaving her cart in front of the door.

"Doris!" My mother shouts from the end of the hallway, she walks quickly with David right behind her. I give her a little smile. "Did you see him? What are they doing now?" She asks, eyeing the closed door.

"He just started barfing everywhere." I blurt out. "It was horrible."

My mother looks both hurt and offended. She huffs at me before pushing aside the cart and entering the room.

"Nicely put Doris." David says chuckling. "Not even sure if mom knows what barf is."

"It was horrible." I repeat and roll my eyes at him. I consider getting up to follow my mother in but I can't will myself up from the chair.

#

(Present)

I push on the arms of my chair to stand but can't seem to get up. I keep trying but I can only lift up an inch or two before I can't get any further.

"Doris, try to stay sitting. You don't want to go back to the hospital. This is your safety belt to keep you from falling again, okay?" A woman is shaking a thick black belt that is loosely secured across my lap.

I nod and pull on the belt. It is really stuck. I wonder what it is stuck on? I follow it with my trembling hands down into the crevice of the seat.

When I lean over I notice the chair has large wheels. Maybe the belt is stuck in the wheels. I lean over and try to push the wheel on one side with both hands. It doesn't move an inch. Maybe because the belt is stuck.

"Here, are you trying to go somewhere Mrs. Atkins? Let me take the breaks off for you." Someone reaches down and pushes a lever in front of the wheel. I feel the chair roll slightly backwards.

How funny. I push the wheel with my hand and I move forward. I lean over further so I can see it turning as I push it. Back and forth, back and forth.

"Hey Mom, what are you doing?"

The familiarity of the voice makes me look up. A dark haired handsome man kneels next to me. My heart swells with love. I give him a smile and pat his hand as it rests on the arm of my chair.

"Are you in trouble? Is that why you're hanging out next to the nurses desk?" He says with a smile and stands up.

I look up at the counter just a few feet from me and see the tops of a few heads. One of them pops up and a woman leans forward on the counter. She scrunches up her nose, "Not Doris! She's never any trouble. Just look at that sweet face."

I don't know what to make of the woman so I give her a half smile and touch my face. This makes the woman laugh loudly and she lowers herself back behind the counter.

"Why don't we take her back to her room where it's more private?" This time a tall blonde woman is speaking. She smiles like she's smelling something stinky.

"Can we go to the game room? Please?" A young curly haired girl chirps as she tugs on the man's hand excitedly.

"Scott, please, I don't like Lana touching a lot of things here. Can we just go your mother's room?" The blonde woman says quietly.

"Honey," says Scott. "It's fine really."

"Maybe we can talk to the guy with the robot voice again, remember that guy?" The girl says with excitement. "Grandma Doris, do you want to go find that robot guy in the game room?"

She reaches over and puts her hand on my arm. Her skin is soft and warm. She's so happy, I want to do whatever she wants to do.

"Yes, yes." I smile.

"See! Grandma wants to go to the game room too!" The girls dark hair bounces with her excitement.

Scott chuckles and leans on the counter, "Excuse me, can you remind us of the name of the gentleman with the electrol-arynx thing. I feel like if we run into him, we shouldn't just call him 'robot guy.'"

Someone behind the counter gives a small laugh, "His name is Cecil but I don't think he'll mind if you called him 'robot guy,' he has a good sense of humor."

"Alright, let's find Cecil!" Lana calls and starts to skip down the hallway.

"Off we go mom, I hope they're doing something fun in the lounge or Lana will be disappointed." Scott starts to push my chair after the girl.

A loud huff and the sound of clicking heels lets me know the blonde lady is following close behind.

I keep my eyes on the girl ahead of me. It seems like with each springy step a sense of joy builds in my chest.

"Aren't we lucky?" I say out loud.

We stop moving and Scott kneels down next to me, "What mom?"

"Aren't we lucky." I repeat.

Scott smiles, "So lucky mom. I love you." Then he leans in and kisses my head.

"So lucky." I repeat.

#

(June 1964)

In the two weeks since my father's funeral, my mother has barely left our house.

"Doris, you know I love your mother but she can't live on

our couch. Can't you talk to her?" Carl has asked me this every night for the last three days. Every night I give him the same response.

"I know, you're right. I'll talk to her tomorrow."

The truth is, when I come home and see her with the kids, I can never find the right moment. I don't know what to say.

"Well you're off tomorrow," he says leaning over to kiss my head. "So maybe I'll take the kids to Ann Arbor with me in the morning. I need to get some clay. That'll give you two some time to talk."

His face says he knows he has me trapped and I'm out of excuses.

"I know I have to do it, you have been so patient," I try to act sweet and pull him in for a long kiss. "Let me thank you." I whisper.

He returns the kiss and pulls me closer.

"I will accept your thanks, but you're not off the hook." He says with a wink.

I give a fake sigh and we soon become tangled together as husband and wife.

In the morning, Carl and the kids load themselves into the car, much to the bewilderment of my mother.

"Why don't you leave the kids here Carl? It will be so much easier for you without them? Do you want me to come along? I can help keep an eye on them?" She has a sort of frantic look in her eyes.

"Mom, you can stay here with me. I could use your help with a few things."

She gives me a suspicious look, because I can count on one hand the number of times I've *asked* for her help with the house.

We wave to the kids as they lean in the rear window, after the car turns the corner my mother calls my bluff.

"Well, they're gone, now what's going on?"

I still haven't figured out what to say, so there's a pause where I let my mouth hang open hoping the words will come if I get the movement started for them.

"Ummm, so, I think you should consider going home." I spit out and immediately realize it sounds too harsh. "So you can check on David, and get back to your sewing, you know... Okay?"

My mother looks out into the yard. I'm not entirely sure of what I have just said, I hope it made some sort of sense.

She stares across the street at the neighbors for so long I start to wonder if I actually said anything at all. I bring my fingers to my mouth to make sure it's not still hanging open.

"I know I should." She says quietly. "Thank you for letting me stay so long.... You really are lucky to have Carl. He's such a good father."

She doesn't look at me. We both stand awkwardly in the summer heat. It occurs to me that this is the type of moment where we should hug but I can't get my body to move towards her. She pats my arm and goes into the house.

She's in the bathroom with the door shut when I come in, I sit at the kitchen table and wait. I start some coffee and return to my post. The clock ticks away the minutes.

What is taking her so long?

"Mom!?" I yell from the kitchen. I wait and hear nothing.

"Mom?" I tap on the door softly. "Mom? You alright?" I think I hear a rustling sound.

"Mom?" I'm speaking loudly now and I pound my fist on the door. "You're scaring me!" I yell and reach for the door handle.

The door swings open just before I touch the knob.

"Why are YOU scared?" She yells.

"*You* aren't alone. You haven't failed your husband. You don't have to go back to a house you know he will never come home to. You aren't the woman who couldn't save her family!" She uses a handfull of toilet paper to wipe her eyes, then pushes past me.

"I'm scared. *I* am the one who is scared!" She stomps her foot and covers her face, lowering herself to the couch.

My mom is not a lady who cries. I've seen her yell and fight. I've seen her stoic and soft. I've seen her face all the gossip of my father's troubles without crumbling. But, even when he disappeared or at the funeral, I never saw a tear.

It takes a conscious effort to do what is so unnatural for us. I sit next to her on the couch and wrap her in my arms.

She leans into me and sobs. I wonder how many times she's cried alone in the last 20 years. I wonder how many times she's hid her face in her pillow or locked herself in the bathroom to keep us from ever seeing her cry.

"You aren't alone mom, even when you go home. We're here for you, so is David. You're not alone. Just let us be here."

It's another moment before she leans out of my embrace. She wipes her face with the soggy toilet paper.

"I love you Doris." I try to meet her gaze.

"I love you too Mom." It's too much, I look away.

#

15

The housekeeper has beautiful red hair. I watch her as she rearranges the photos on the window sill. It reminds me of someone.

"Have you ever met my mother?" I ask abruptly. She pauses her work briefly, then continues.

"Yes, I remember Grandma McArthur." She answers with a slight question in her voice.

"Grandma? You must be thinking of another McArthur. But I wanted to say you remind me of her, well at least your hair. It's the same shade."

"Really?" the woman turns around so I can see all her features. She's very familiar looking. She must come here a lot.

"Mom, in all my memories of Grandma McArthur most of her hair was grey. It didn't hold it's red tint like yours does." I touch my own hair and pull a few locks into view. It looks course and rusty.

A broad smile lights the woman's face and she laughs a familiar laugh. "She was a wonderful grandmother. She could be a little pushy and she liked a tidy house but she was the best grandma."

My mother is her grandma? I smile and consider this for a moment then it becomes more than I can grasp. I picture my mother in her fifties, helping out around my house.

Images of Suzy and Scott flash through my mind as well, with their pudgy cheeks and messy hands. I try to remember the last time I saw them. Searching for the thought is like tugging at a lead curtain in my mind. I can't budge it and the effort is exhausting. I close my eyes briefly.

When I open them the young woman is still talking to me although I can't make out what she's saying. Her hair is a beautiful shade of red. The talking stops and the woman stares at me as if she's expecting a response so I say the first thing that comes to mind.

"How nice dear, you know my mother had red hair just like yours."

#

(December 1964)

"Mom, why do you go to work?" Scott and Suzy sit at the end of the bed watching me get ready. They look so sweet in their cowboy themed pajamas.

"So we can pay the bills and put food on the table. Right, babe?" Carl says as he slaps my bottom before he gets his socks from the drawer.

"Well, Mikey Sherman says that is why *Dads* go to work but I'm the only one in my class whose *Mom* works everyday. He says we must be a commune-ist because you work and Dad stays home." Scott says with concern. "Are we a commune-ist?"

Carl bursts into laughter and I give him a look. He turns away and tries to contain himself.

In the past year I have rarely been uncertain about Carl and I's decision to trade roles.

I know some other mothers consider me neglectful and I've heard through the grapevine that I have been diagnosed as "mentally ill" in some circles. At least with all the buzz of the *Feminine Mystique*, I have hope that some people might see why it works for us.

For the most part, I couldn't care less, but I've been dreading the time when my children would have to answer for our decisions.

I kneel down so I can look at both of their faces because I want them both to understand what I want to tell them.

"Mommy works because she likes it. I like working in a factory and building cars. It makes me feel happy. Your Daddy is an artist. He works at home creating sculptures and carvings that people like and want to put in their homes because that is what makes him feel happy." I pause to glance at Carl, he is attentively listening now too.

"We're both doing what we need to, to take care of our whole family, including ourselves. We are not communists. We are doing things a little different but there isn't anything wrong with that. Do you understand?"

Suzy nods and Scott looks at me skeptically.

"If other people- kids or adults - are worried about what *we* are doing in our family, it's because *they* are probably scared, or unhappy, or just not as brave as us. Okay?"

Scott tilts his head, "So we are not commune-ists, we're brave because you work, right Mommy?"

"Yes, baby, we are brave." I kiss his cheek.

"Then Mikey and his Dad are just scaredy cats!"He jumps off the bed and runs through the house yelling "scaredy cats, scaredy cats!"

Carl starts to laugh again, "I think he got the important parts."

"I sure hope so." I say pulling on my work shirt.

#

(Present)

The screaming is so horrible I drop my fork and cover my ears. How long are they going to let him scream?

"Call the ambulance! Call the ambulance!" I yell to the crowded room, no one seems to be moving.

"Mrs. Atkins, please calm down. It's okay." A small familiar woman grabs my hands and squeezes them.

"He's still screaming, call the ambulance, please!" I beg the woman.

"It's just Leon, honey. He's just got to yelling, he's not hurt. It's okay." She looks at me with concern. Unlocking my chair, she moves me away from the table. She points to a man in a wheelchair with his head flung back letting out a mournful yell. "See, he's fine, he just hollers sometimes."

My mind plays a different image though. It flashes in and out. I can still hear the man screaming. His leg will be all bloody when they bring him up from the bay. The gears have almost tore his leg clear off, and he just keeps screaming.

"His leg, call the ambulance! Please call the ambulance." I grab at the hand of the yelling man as I'm pushed by him. "Please, call."

We push through two double doors into a brightly lit hallway. It looks festive with red bows hanging on the walls. I wring my hands in my lap.

"Please, call. Please, call." I whisper to myself.

"Doris, look at me." The woman is kneeling down with her

hands on mine, she gently tilts my head so our eyes meet. "Look right here Doris. Shhh, do you hear that?"

I listen, there is music. It sounds familiar. It reminds me of a gathering. Maybe a party. My hands stop wringing, the gripping tightness in my chest releases.

"It's a party." I say to the woman.

"It's Christmas music." The woman replies and gives me a smile, "And it's Christmas Eve, Mrs. Atkins."

I think about Christmas Eve and picture a fat Santa with a bag of gifts. "Well, I guess we better get to bed then, right?" I wonder if my family is having Christmas somewhere. My hands take back up their wringing.

"I guess you're right." She says and she starts singing along with the music. "Do you know this song Doris? My mom used to love this song."

"Ding-dong, Ding-dong, Hear the bell…"

"Is this the Vandella's?" She continues to hum along then does a little dance next to my chair.

I laugh, the Supremes flash through my mind. I can see Diana Ross belting the tune. "No, no, no." I say.

"Huh, I thought you would have known this one, it's a classic." She pats my hand again and we start moving down the hall.

The song continues in my head as I watch my hands circle each other in my lap. She doesn't understand.

"Ding Dong, Ding Dong…" I sing as we move.

"That's it Doris, you do remember!" she makes my chair do a little dance in the hall and I let out a laugh.

I raise my hand, she stops the chair and kneels next to me again.

"Diana Ross." The name found its way to my lips.

"Good job Doris!" She gives me a high five. "It is Diana Ross, The Supremes, I should have known."

I clap and bob my head as we continue down the hall singing.

"Ding, dong, ding, dong, ding….."

#

(March 1965)

The factory closed up for a week or so due to high inventory before the spring buying season. It was good timing for us because Carl had been chomping at the bit to join the marches in Alabama.

We finally came to an agreement, he could go for a week with a group heading down from Detroit and he would be back before I had to return to work.

"Dad, can I please come and march with you? I'm great at marching and I won't even whine if it's a long drive." Scott begs, while demonstrating his marching skills up and down the hallway.

"I love that you want to come, it shows what a big heart you have son." Carl kisses the top of Scotts head. "I'll take you when you're older. Marching can be dangerous, I need you to take care of your sister and mom while I'm gone, okay?"

Once Scott resolves himself to being left behind, he begins to take his new responsibility as "man of the house" very seriusly. He spends our first evening without Carl designing booby traps to warn off intruders. I have since stubbed my toe on full cans of beans stacked in front of my room and almost broke my neck tripping over string and bell lined doorways.

The weather is still cold but the snow has mostly melted to mud leaving only grey speckled mounds along the sidewalks. For the second time today I'm washing a pair of pants Scott has soaked playing outside without his snow gear on.

He's restricted to watching TV in his underwear because I told him he was done outside and his only option was to put on his pajamas. Hanging out in his underwear is his sort of protest to inviting an early bedtime.

"Grandma is going to be here any minute, are you going to greet her in your underwear?"

"She's grandma, she doesn't care." He says defiantly.

"Alright," I sigh, pause and fake surprise. "Oh, here she is now coming up the walk!"

Scott gets up and runs to the hallway. I laugh, "Gotcha! I knew you didn't want Grandma to see your undies!"

"Mom!" Scott whines then stomps to his room.

I pick Suzy up from the floor, "Oh, girl, you are getting too big!" I carry her to her room to get her changed.

Just as I pull Suzy's nightgown over her head, I hear my mother come in the door.

With one of her arms still lost in her nightgown, Suzy wrestles herself away from me and runs out to find my mother.

"Gramma's here! Gramma's here!" she yells.

Scott zooms past the door to greet her.

I follow them both out and the three are snuggled into a group embrace at the front door.

"Thanks for coming Mom." I say as I put on my coat. I won't be too long. I just need to get a few groceries.

She leans in and gives my cheek a peck. She's been more affectionate since my dad died. I'm getting used to it now.

"Don't worry, take your time." She calls over her shoulder as she's led away by two giggling children.

At the market I run into a few wives of some of the men I work with. My least favorite part of grocery shopping is the small talk.

"When do you think you'll get back to work? John, is so bored at home." I give this one a polite smile.

"Are you enjoying all this time you *finally* get with your kids?" I meet her insincere smile with an excessively animated nod and an internal eye roll.

"I don't know how you keep it together with Carl in the middle of all that mess. I mean I know he's trying to help but, aren't you worried because of what happened last time?" This one gets a combination polite smile-nod with an internal eye roll and the only acceptable verbal response that won't lead to more questions. "I have faith."

That response is a cop out considering I haven't been to church since the funeral but it's not untrue. I do have faith that either God or Carl can keep him out of trouble for the next four days. He's been warned not to touch any property or signs of any sort and that if he ends up in jail, he's going to have to get himself out then answer to me.

I figure I'm doing my part for the civil rights movement by letting him go and keeping things running while he is gone.

On the way home I decide to treat myself to a shake at the Chick-Inn diner. I pull in under its angled roof and press the intercom button, needing to shout my order for a peanut butter banana milkshake through a crackling speaker.

I'm parked in the spot next to the large window of the small dining area inside the building. The table closest to me has a couple holding hands deep in conversation. The woman leans over and kisses the man across from her, as she sits back down the gentleman's face becomes clear and familiar.

Our eyes meet and the surprise of seeing each other leaves us both unabashedly staring.

The young woman turns to follow Paul's gaze. I look away quickly. I start to fumble through my purse to get my money ready so I can leave as soon as my shake comes out. I'm startled by a tap on the window and afraid to look up. What if it's Paul? The tapping persists but it is only a skinny teenager trying not to freeze while she serves my shake in a too tight sweater.

"Oh, sorry, thank you." I say as I crank the window down and hand her a $1 bill.

"Let me get your change." She fumbles with the coin dispenser on her waist and quarters roll onto the pavement. "Oh, sorry, my hands are totally frozen, hang on ma'am."

She pops back up into the window to hand me my change. I tuck it into my purse and begin to crank the window back up when I hear him.

"Doris?"

I consider pretending I don't hear him. I could continue to roll up the window, peel out of here and never look back.

But then there he is, standing in front of my car. I glance back to the table where he was sitting and find it's empty.

I give him a smile. He returns a small wave then shoves his hands deep into the pockets of his long wool coat. His hair is short and combed to the right. He still looks handsome, still like Paul Newman.

I'm not sure what to do. Should I get out, should I leave. Is he going to come to the window, should I roll it down. Neither of us move, we just stare. After a minute a car honks from a few spots down. Paul waves again, I smile, then he jogs through the slush over to the car.

I watch him get in and they pull out onto Holmes Rd. I don't look away until the tail lights are lost amongst the others on the road and I know he's gone.

I exhale loudly and start the car, now that there is a safe distance between us. I let myself think about Paul a little and find myself smiling on the way home. I tap my thumb on the steering wheel as Blueberry Hill plays softly on the radio.

#

16

The hand wags in my lap. It seems to be moving faster, thumb leading the way back and forth, back and forth.

There are small blue dots on my pants that are not supposed to be there. I touch one with my finger, it moves. I pinch and pull it off my pants to inspect it. It's soft, fuzzy. I drop it to the side then pick up the next one and inspect it. It's soft and fuzzy. I drop it to the side. I watch my thumb shake.

There are sounds in the background, music and voices. "We may want to mention to the doctor that the tremors are getting worse again and she seems zoned out. Maybe he can adjust her Risperidone."

Suddenly I'm moving, the tiles pass quickly under my chair, then there's carpet and I stop. A box with a black and white photo appears in my lap. I look up slowly and make eye contact with a thin young black woman. Somehow I see her mouth moving before I hear her words.

"We - are - going - to - watch - a - movie!" She yells at me then taps the thin box in my lap. A photo of a handsome young man is on the box with a few other faces.

"

I lift my wagging hand and tap on the man's face. I know him, I think to myself. My hand continues to tap at an uncontrolled rhythm on the box. He is so familiar. My heart races and I feel warmth.

"P-P-p-p-p..." I pull my lips together and look up at the woman again. She is waiting patiently.

I look back down at the face my finger is still drumming. "P-P-P-t.....P-P-Paauull." I get out in a gritty voice that startles me.

The woman kneels down and looks from me to the picture. "Paul?" She exclaims. "That's right Doris, It's Paul Newman! See he's too handsome to forget?" She giggles.

No. I think. My Paul. I tap my chest and try to get the words out again. "P-P-Pauull!" I say loudly this time looking meaningfully at the aide.

"That's right Mrs. Doris, he gets my heart going too." She taps her chest and takes the box from me.

I look around the room and see a few people scattered about, all are facing a large television mounted on the wall. A woman is pushes buttons on a small box just underneath the television.

"Time for *Cool Hand Luke* everyone!" She claps a couple times then steps out of view. I'm surprised to see that I have started to clap as well. In a few moments a familiar face fills the screen. "P-P-P-P-p-pt-pa-pl-pl..." I hear myself stuttering.

#

(March 1965)

I don't mention to my mother that I saw Paul at the Chick-Inn, although I wonder what he's doing in town.

Is he still here, is he visiting someone? The last I heard he was back in Indianapolis and I haven't heard anything about him since. I thought he was gone, we were over, nothing to worry about. It makes me wish Carl were here.

A couple days before Carl is supposed to be back I try to see if my mother knows anything, without raising her suspicions.

While she scrubs at a casserole dish in the sink, I pretend to read one of Carl's old newspapers. I've planted this one on the table specifically because it mentions Indianapolis.

"Oh, it looks like that race down in Indianapolis is going to be a big deal this year. All the guys at work keep talking about the British cars." I say keeping my eyes on the paper.

"Paul used to talk about cars a lot," I lie but look up to watch her reaction at the mention of Paul. "I wonder if he goes to those races since he lives so close?"

My mothers scrubbing slows, she gazes out the window for a moment then returns to scrubbing with increased vigor.

"Have you heard?" I ask watching her.

"What?" she asks in a mumble.

"About the races, or about Paul...I haven't heard anything about him lately." I can tell she knows something.

After a short silence she answers. "Well, he's in town if that's what you're asking at." She flings her washcloth into the water and turns to face me. She puts her soapy hands on her hips and plants her feet wide like she's ready to fight.

"He's supposed to be getting married to a girl he met in Indiana. I figured there was no reason for you to care so I didn't bother telling you." She says, half yelling at me and half scolding me.

"Well alright then," I half yell back at her. "I didn't do anything wrong with asking."

I huff a little and turn back to the paper on the table. I feel like I'm in high school again.

Why does she have to be like that? I don't care if Paul's getting married, good for him. It's what I wanted for him. To be happy, and move on. Right? There's blank static in my head. My stomach has tightened up, a dull ache moves across my chest. I breathe deeply. A lump in my throat? Am I going to cry? This is crazy. Paul has been out of my life for so long. I am happy for him. I *am* happy for him.

I clear my throat and take a drink of water. "I'm happy for him." I say matter of factly.

My mother has gone back to washing the dishes. "Good." she says sternly.

"Good." I say back then get up from the table and go to my room. Our room. Carl and I's room.

Crawling into Carl's side of the bed, I let the earthy smell that lingers on him after he works with clay fill my nose. I pull his pillow close and stare into the bright light from the window. I press my face into the fabric and the tears come.

I feel lonely.

I miss him.

#

(Present)

There are two or three people standing in front of the window. I can only make out their silhouettes through my half closed lids but I their voices are clear.

"So is he going to come back and visit her?" A female voice

is asking.

"He didn't say. It's so weird." A male voice responds, "I guess I understand it, but it just isn't like him."

"What! How can you understand leaving her, abandoning her! She's your mother!" Another female voice, deeper and more emotional than the first.

"But it's been so long, and he's still alive and healthy. If she were gone…Ow, geez."

The sound of a slap on fabric then the deeper female voice interrupts. "She is right-fucking-there Scott! She's not dead."

A sobbing sound fills the room and one of the silhouettes lowers into a chair. Another silhouette merges with it. I can see them better now, without the window light behind them, a blonde woman holding a red haired woman. The man remains standing.

"I know, I'm sorry. I'm just saying that I know he loves her, it's hard for him. He's lonely. You should hear him talk about her. He has been mourning her since she moved out. He didn't want to be alone anymore. I'm just not judging him, that's all." The man shuffles in place.

All three of them stand again, their voices are lowered and muffled. There is hugging. I'm happy to see them hugging.

"Well what are you smiling at!" The red haired woman exclaims when her eyes meet mine.

I didn't realize was smiling but I can feel it widen across my face now.

"Mom, are you feeling rested?" The man bends over and rubs my shoulder, tilting his head. His tilting makes me aware that I am lying on my side in bed and I'm surprised by this.

I should get up, I have guests.

I try to get up but my body is unorganized causing my arm

and legs to jerk forward wildly.

"Whoa, sorry to startle you Mom!" The man says stepping back with his hand raised.

"Can I help you sit up?" The red haired woman kneels down.

I nod. She puts her hands behind my knees and pulls my legs to the edge of the bed.

"Now, push yourself up okay?" She squats near my legs. Her words bounce around in my head, trying to find meaning.

"Mom, push up with your arms." She motions with her arms and mimics her elbow pushing to the side. I stare intently then feel my elbow pushing into the bed. Soon I'm sitting up with my feet barely touching the floor.

"Hi Doris, how are you feeling today!?" the blonde woman yells with exaggerated nodding, her big blonde hair bounces with each nod. It's almost white in the light from the window. I feel my head nod along with hers.

"Laurie, you don't have to yell, talking louder isn't going to make her understand. Her hearing is fine." The man says in a gentle tone as he squeezes her hand.

The blonde pulls her lips back with a half grimace, "Sorry, I just forget."

The redhead looks at me and rolls her eyes, "Can we get you into your chair Mom?" She gives me a big smile.

Something in her face reminds me of someone.

"Where's Carl?" My voice is hoarse and I'm a little surprised by the ease of the words. It appears everyone else is surprised as well.

Raised eyebrows and looks are exchanged, but instead of an answer I am presented with my slippers and a "let's get ready for the day."

#

(March 1965)

"What do you mean you aren't coming home?" I can barely stop myself from yelling through the phone at Carl, the kids just went to bed and I don't want to wake them up.

"Babe, really no one is heading back. Things are moving, there are some student groups who are organizing everything. The President is actually responding. He pushed congress last week and now we might get to really make the march to the capital!" Carl sounds all jazzed up like he used to before Scott was born.

"No! Didn't some people get beat to death a few weeks ago doing that? What is the matter with you? Come home. You chipped in, you helped the cause, but now we need you home." I can't even try to keep my voice down anymore so I stretch the phone cord as far away from the kids rooms as I can and stand almost in the dining room.

A long silence hangs between us. Then a strange voice on the line, "You guys almost done here, this isn't a private line you know. A lot of guys are waiting to call from over here too."

"Yeah, just a minute. Sorry babe, this phone is a party line for the block." Carl says quietly.

"But if you could feel it Doris, it's electric here, then you'd understand." I hear him take a breath. "I can't leave yet though. I don't have a ride but I probably wouldn't go if I did. I'm sorry. I love you all but this is bigger than us. It's big and it's good."

I sit on the floor in the middle of the kitchen, everything seems so unfair. "Fine Carl." I say barely above a whisper. "I hope it's worth it."

"It is, it won't be long. Don't be mad, I love you babe."

The stranger's voice is back, "Sorry, man, times up."

It takes a minute before I can stand. I hang the phone back in its cradle then pick it up and slam it down again. Hot angry tears stream down my cheeks. I just want him home. I don't want to be alone here anymore, how does he not get it?

I am mad.

I'm mad that now I have to call and ask more favors from my mother. I'm mad that he's making me miss him. I'm mad that he's making me feel vulnerable. I'm mad because now I feel guilty and selfish for having any feelings at all because he is trying to help other people. It's just not fair.

I gave a week, willingly, why did he have to take more?

I try not to care about what other people say but they will talk. He's gone again, rumors will start. Isn't he thinking about us? What if he *is* arrested again, or hurt or killed? Is it worth it?

I wonder if this is how my mother felt when my father would disappear? Alone, wondering if he's safe, if we're safe? I know it's different in so many ways but right now it feels the same.

#

(Present)

I hear people laughing just outside the open door.

"She is so ridiculous!" One voice says and the laughing continues. More voices join in but I can't make out what they're saying.

Why are they laughing? Are they laughing at me?

I push up from my chair but am stopped by a belt. They have me tied down.The chair rolls backwards with my movements. I can still move though. I use my feet to push myself forward and my arms to pull myself along the bed towards the doorway. When I make it to the hallway three women wearing matching colored scrubs are standing a few feet from my door.

"Good afternoon Doris." One of them chirps. They all smile wide grins in my direction. Are they mocking me?

I stare at them, the anger growing slowly. Why wouldn't people just leave me alone. I'm always being talked about and laughed at. I'm a good person, I try to do the right things. Did they know? That must be it, they knew.

"Just stop it!" I yell with spit flying from my lips. "Stop, stop, stop!"

I'm trembling with anger and waving my hand at them.

"Oh, Doris, we're so sorry. What did we do?" A tall brunette with a high ponytail bends down and pats my leg.

How condescending, she wouldn't fool me.

"You can't judge, you aren't God!" I point to the ceiling and they all look up. My voice is wavering, phlegm gathers in my throat. "You aren't..." I trail off and start to cough.

"Let me get her." A small woman waves the trio off and kneels beside me as I continue to cough. She pulls out a couple tissues and puts them in my flailing hand then pushes it in front of my mouth. I see her name tag reads Faye.

"Are you alright Mrs. Atkins? Can I get you some water?" Her face looks honestly concerned.

I shake my head no and clear my throat a few times. I feel agitated but I'm not sure why. I stare at the woman next to me, I don't think I'm mad at her.

The anger grows with my confusion. I feel my face flush, I want to yell or do something but since I don't know why I'm mad I don't know how to fix it. I start to shred the tissues in my lap.

"It looks like you're mad about something." She says putting her hand over mine.

Nodding, I look her in the eye, glad that she understands.

Her eyes get wide with surprise, "Whooo, I guess so Mrs. Atkins, and I wouldn't want to be on your bad side!" She starts to laugh. Her smile makes me smile and the weight in my chest lightens.

"There, now, I love to see that beautiful smile!"

I relax I putting my hand over hers.

"It's alright Doris, you can be be mad if you want to. No one has to be happy all the time."

I take another deep breath, tears form at the corner of my eyes. The emotions have to go somewhere.

I squeeze her hand tightly, she squeezes back. I let the tears fall and feel relieved.

#

17

Scott jumps up and down squeezing both my hands.

"I can't believe you're going to miss this Mom! And Dad too!" Scott is beside himself with excitement waiting for the Gemini launch that would be televised after school.

"I know, I'm sad about it too but you and Grandma can tell me all about it at dinner after work, okay?" I pick him up and kiss his cheek.

"Mom! Stop! I'm too big for you to carry me!" He wiggles from my arms and wipes his face.

"Well then come and kiss your mother goodbye like a gentleman." I say kneeling down and tapping my cheek. He rolls his eyes and gives me a quick peck before running off to his room.

"Good luck with him today." I give my mother a half smile. "He's full of it."

"He'll be fine, a boy should get excited. These are exciting times." She replies frowning. "It's a nice break from the news of the war and that mess Carl is into in Alabama."

"Yeah, don't remind me. I talked to him for a minute last night, he says it's safe because of the National Guard troops the President sent there I guess."

I rub my forehead and sigh. "I still can't believe he's doing this. I can't even tell him how angry I am because, what if….you know…something happens…" I get a lump in my throat and turn to find my boots.

"Don't worry Doris. Carl is crazy for putting you through all this but he loves you guys. He'll be okay. He's on the right side of this fight." She pats my shoulder a couple times. "And besides, you can give him hell when he gets home."

I give her a little smile. "No doubt I will."

I review the situation in my head for the hundredth time. If he's back in a week I'll be lucky.

Please let him get home safe, just get him home safe. I seem to have this constant chant running through my mind. It's heartfelt, exhausting and annoying. I need a break, but I have no place to go.

"David wanted me to remind you about tonight, too. That will be something to distract you." She gives me a smile and hands me my lunch.

I almost forgot about David.

In the car I try to organize the day in my head. I'll have to hurry after work to get back home and change so I can meet David at the restaurant.

He made me promise I would go out with him for his birthday, which was two weeks ago. I'm guessing our mother put him up to it because he's been really persistent.

I try not to feel pathetic that my mom is organizing pity social outings for me with my brother and focus on the fact that I'm getting out.

It's become obvious I don't have any actual friends anymore. I used to have a few neighborhood ladies I could play cards with but they've all distanced themselves to acquaintances since Carl and I got back together.

It's sort of understandable, our routines don't mesh and neither do our roles. I'm at work with their husbands and when I'm off they are at home getting dinner ready and taking care of their families.

Guilt creeps into my mind as I think about the burned dinners Carl has prepared and how much my mother has done for our family.

Am I really doing the best thing for them by not being there? I do enjoy working but I can't help but wonder if I'm being selfish, what sort of example will I prove to be?

I consider trying to bail on David tonight, he probably won't mind. I'll call him after work, I should spend more time at home.

#

(Present)

Paul is holding me tight and we are dancing. He starts to turn me, then shake me, I'm falling and reach out but he slaps away my hand.

My eyes jerk open and the round freckled face of an aide comes into focus. Her voice is loud and her hand shakes my hip, a sharp pain runs up my back. I reach down to slap away her arm.

"Now don't get mad at me Mrs. Atkins. You can't be slappin' at people and you can't stay in bed all day." The woman is still too loud but has stopped shaking me.

I don't want to get out of bed. I don't recognize this woman or the room behind her. I see a few items that look familiar but nothing registers. I close my eyes.

The shaking starts again at my hip and the sharp pain returns.Without opening my eyes I swat her hand again and try to roll over.

"Doris!" the loud voice booms in the small room. "You can't be hitting. I'll have to tell the doctor that you're gettin' more agitated. Maybe he can give you something to relax."

She huffs and I hear her rustling around in the room. A few moments later the door creaks open and noises from outside drift in. I hear her talking in the hallway.

"Gail, she's gonna need to be changed from a mod assist x1 to a max assist x2 in these charts. If she's going to be hittin' people and refusing to get up then it's going to take more than one person to move her."

"Just note it there in the computer, Beth. I'll review it with the care team tomorrow. I think she's going downhill so a few other things will need changed too."

Another voice answers the loud woman. "Just give me a sec and I'll come in to help you with her."

I squeeze my eyelids tight. White spots drift across the black like snowflakes. I shiver and my body relaxes. I see snowflakes falling into Carl's dark hair. I reach my hand up to dust one from his thick lashes. He looks at me and smiles, then winks.

THere is a loud voice, "Doris, we're going to roll you over and sit you up so we can get you into your chair for lunch!"

Then I'm rolling. My eyes flutter open to see a blur of white ceiling and faces. I feel my legs flail.

"Well, we got you awake now, right Doris!" One of the women chuckles as the blankets are pulled off me.

When my head catches up with my body, I'm settled on my side, a round freckled face pops into view just inches from the edge of the bed.

"We are going to sit you up now Doris. Can you help us sit you up!" She is nodding and smiling encouragingly.

All I can register is how loud she is. I know she wants something from me but things are moving too fast. It seems every time I get a thought in my head something else happens and I lose it. I stare back at her intently, waiting for understanding.

I feel hands on my legs and more on my shoulders. The freckled faced woman is hovering closely over me.

"One, two, three!" And I am being thrust upright, I feel my legs falling from the edge of the bed. My arms shoot out protectively, slapping the woman in her freckles and grabbing tightly to her shoulder. My nails sink into skin as I try to anchor myself from the movement.

"Oh, shit. Doris, relax, relax ...Gail get her hand, get her hand ..." The freckled face woman is speaking quickly but much quieter than before. Her lips are pursed and her face is turning red. The other woman pries my hand from her shoulder. I try to relax as she places my hand on the edge of the bed to help steady me.

The first woman exhales loudly. "Oh, thanks. I think I lost some skin there and I might be getting a fat lip. Let's get her in the chair and I'll go check myself out." The two women exchange looks. "I might have to fill out an incident report. At least you were here."

Gail lifts up the arm of the wheelchair and scoots it in close, then wraps a thick green belt around my waist. The freckle faced woman holds the chair steady and guides my hips while Gail lifts up on the belt pulling me off the bed. I feel my legs engage and soon we are pivoting toward the chair.

"Atta girl Doris. Get some use of those legs!" Gail says as

we turn and I'm lowered into the seat. The arm of the chair is replaced and a buckle is secured across my lap. "Atta girl," She repeats.

The freckled woman pulls her shirt down her shoulder and touches the red blood surfacing through the scratches on her skin. " Do you need me to send someone else in here? I need to go get this cleaned up."

"No, I got this. Your lip is swelling a bit too. You should probably ice it." Gail responds. "You need to be more gentle Doris." she scolds.

I look from her to the woman with the swollen lip. I again feel like they want something from me but I can't put any of it together.

I reach out to hold each of their hands with my trembling fingers. Their fingers are warm in my hands and I squeeze. "Dear Lord," I say in a whisper. "Atta girl, atta girl."

They return my squeeze and laugh a little.

A loud voice replies,"That's right Mrs. Atkins, that's al-right."

#

(March 1965)

I'm a little late meeting David at the Sidetrack for a drink and dinner. My mom wouldn't let me cancel and I haven't tried to "go out" in so long I couldn't figure out what to wear. I even borrowed a bright purple scarf to tie around my neck from my mom because she said it would "wake up my face," whatever that means. I decided to push aside the guilt and try to have fun. If Carl could take weeks off from responsibility I could take a night.

"So nice of you to join me Mrs. Atkins." David teases jo-vially when I find him seated at a table, already halfway through his drink. He looks a little uncomfortable and out of place with his hair hanging over his ears and his chin sunk into his heavy brown jacket.

"Sorry, David. I didn't know how to dress. I realized I haven't been out in ages. I don't have a clue what people wear when they aren't in a factory or cleaning up after children."

"I'm flattered by your desire to impress me." He says with mock Clark Gable intonation. "But you needn't have worried yourself madam."

I roll my eyes and plop into the seat across from him.

He straightens up and pushes a short glass filled with a brown liquor and ice towards me. "So sis, I ordered you a drink. How about you try to relax."

"Sounds perfect." I take a sip from the cold glass and my throat immediately begins to burn.

I try to stifle a cough. "What is this?"

"Bourbon." He answers cooly and takes a sip of his drink.

"Do you think I'm James Bond or something? This is horrible."

He laughs and takes my glass, emptying it into his. "That's a Martini, not bourbon. I just thought it might get you loosened up quicker, you are usually all high strung."

I squint at him, "I'm not high strung, I'm just busy!" I take a sip from his glass without coughing this time, just to make a point.

He smirks and pushes the water towards me.

We sit in slightly awkward silence for a few minutes.

"But man, if you wanted to have fun we should've gone out to Detroit to the Hullabaloo. They have a great band tonight."

He looks wistful, the way he always does when he talks

about music. My mother complains that all he does is sit and play records with his friends. Since he quit the factory, he's been working down at Von's Market a few days a week but he doesn't seem to be making any plans for his future.

"Don't call me "man," and Mom would kill us, AND I have kids so I can't go out all night like a teenager." I immediately hate every word.

"Ugh, I'm old." I put my elbows on the table and cradle my head. "And definitely uptight."

"You're not really that old. I mean what are you 25?" He takes a long swig of his beer. "And I didn't know you cared what people thought."

I give him a long hard look.

"Don't take it bad, I'm just saying you always sort of do your own thing. Not totally crazy like, but not walking the line either."

He lights a cigarette and gives me a smile. "Let me take you out to Hullabaloo, The Rationals are playing and they are really boss, man. You'll love it."

"You're nuts." I shake my head at him. He gives me an encouraging smile.

Why not? I think to myself. I haven't been to a club in years and he's right, I'm not that old. Lord knows Carl is probably out drinking and having fun.

"Fine I'll go, but take this dime and *you* call Mom to let her know. She won't give you a hard time, you're her *baby*." He gives me a look that lets me know I'm being a total "square."

"I'll be cool if you do me this one last favor okay?" I say and push the dime closer.

"It's a deal, sis." He flips the dime in the air and heads off to find a payphone.

I look around at the crowd in the Sidetrack. It's mostly people in their 30's or older, out for a respectable evening, couples or groups of couples chat and laugh together. They'll probably be home in an hour or two just after their children were tucked safely in bed by teenage sitters. A table with three men, looking fresh from an office, are the most rowdy and it's only because they keep loudly shaking their empty glasses at their waitress.

David is right, this was not the place for a night out.

The door opens sending a blast of cold air through the bar that ruffles my napkin. A lone figure in the doorway takes off his hat and slaps it on his leg to brush the snow off. It feels like a scene from Gunsmoke.

"Holy Shit." I think, or maybe say out loud.

It's Paul.

Of course it is, I laugh to myself.

The office men wave and whistle toward him, and I think I might be able to get out of here without him seeing me if David hurries up.

Their table is a few away from ours but not between us and the door. Paul walks to the table wearing a handsome boyish grin. He slings his coat and chevron knitted scarf over his forearm, when he's almost reached his table, David plows right into him.

David is distracted, eyeing a young blonde waitress and nearly knocks Paul into the lap of an older gentleman at nearby. Luckily, the gentleman has one hand free and is able to push Paul back to his feet.

"Aw, man, sorry, man, really…...Paul?"

"David?" Paul smiles. "How are you?" He gives him a hearty handshake.

"Just move on, please." I let the thought repeat like a prayer in my brain.

The guys from the table are still calling to Paul, he raises a finger for them to wait. I can't hear what they're talking about and Paul's back is to me. I consider ducking under the table or running to the bathroom.

I need to relax. Paul and I are over, I need to be able to act normal around him or people will think something's still going on. I take another drink of David's bourbon and wait for the inevitable.

David points at me, Paul turns to look. I give a little smile. Will he come over here? Paul waves back, our eyes lock for a moment. My heart races, he steps towards our table but only to make room for David to pass through.

When he gets to his table he's greeted with a slap on the back and some chuckles. His friends push out the two open seats at the table. Paul picks the chair with his back to me.

For some reason, it hurts a little.

"Paul's here for a bachelor party, I guess they're just getting dinner before they head out to party." David says when he returns to the table. "Seeing him is so weird. It seems like ages ago you guys were together."

I nod, half listening, my throat is dry. I sip my water. David is oblivious to my discomfort.

"Mom, told me not to get you into trouble but I don't think she cares about us being out later. So I'll just pay for this," He takes a long drink of the bourbon. "And we can grab a bite when we get there."

I pick up the glass and down the rest. "Let's go." I say abruptly.

Is that tightness in my throat the bourbon?

The quicker I get out of here, the better.

#

(Present)

The lines go up and down and up and down. The knitting is beautiful, but loosened. So many colors, up and down, up and down.

This is called something. I poke at the lines in my lap. I trace them up and down with my finger. The yarn is thick. My brain spins looking for words. Pictures come to mind. The store with Carl's mother. Hanging these for display.

My brain is still searching. Thick balls of yarn at my mother's feet. Sheets of lines go up and down. So many colors. My finger retraces the path, up and down.

Scott with pudgy cheeks under these lines, under this yarn. Suzy dragging this behind her through the house giving her bunny a ride. I poke my finger through a loose hole.

Pictures of Carl's mother's store again, a sign hangs. "Afghans are a family treasure. Try a new pattern today." Afghans, that sounds right. I feel my lips move. A slight breath passes through them as I try to make the word. "Afghan," I whisper.

Someone near me is talking. Two voices, the rhythm of their conversation is interrupted when I find my voice.

"Afghan." I say and feel the vibration through my throat and mouth. It's a nice feeling, my teeth brush my bottom lip. It is dry and rough. I bring my hand from the blanket to my lips and feel the word as it leaves my mouth. "Afghan." I hold onto the last sound and let the vibration fill the back of my throat.

"Mom? Mom." A pretty woman kneels next to me and touches my chin. "Lift up your head. Lift it up." She pushes up with two fingers and I raise my head to see her eyes, a beautiful green. She smiles and I feel happiness so I smile back.

A much older man is standing next to her. His grey hair is long and stringy, it hangs to his shoulders. His hands are buried in the pockets of loose jeans. He gives me a half smile.

My mind searches for him briefly before I give up and smile back. I trust the closeness I feel with these two.

"Mom, your brother David is here from California to see you." She raises her eyebrows and points to the long haired man.

"Hey Sis," he says. His voice cracks and he turns away. He clears his throat then points to the recliner next to me, "Mind if I sit here." Not waiting for an answer, he sits.

I keep my eyes on him, waiting for him to give me the clue that will bring his memory from where it hides in my mind.

"She's having more trouble with words lately. Sometimes she can get out a sentence, sometimes it's just sounds…" The woman trails off. "Depends on the day…"

His eyes are water, he reaches over and puts his hand in mine. I know I love him. I put my hand on his.

"I'm David, your little brother, man." He says and shakes my hand. "Remember you used to keep on my ass when we came home from school to make sure I did my homework and finished my chores? You weren't gonna let me slack off if Mom wasn't around. Remember that?"

I can see on his face that he wants me to remember. I smile and pat his hand. "David." I whisper hoarsely, although I cannot place the name.

"Yes!" He looks relieved. "Remember the time I came home from school and had ripped the knees out of the pants Mom had just made me? You were sweeping and whacked me in the arm with the broom!" He slaps his knee.

"I had a bruise and everything, but I couldn't tell on you

because you were going to patch them up for me before mom noticed. You would always try to keep me out of trouble."

I have a vision of me mending a navy pair of trousers in the kitchen. A sour faced boy with reddish blonde hair holds his arm and watches me. He's wearing a striped T-shirt and his underwear.

"Good grief, David, at least put on some play pants. Mom's going to ask questions if you're running around in just undies!"

It clicks and I look from the image of the little boy in my mind to the old hippie in the recliner. Were they the same?

"Good grief, David." I mumble, forcing the words from my mind to my lips."Ppput'n your pants."

"Yes! Yes!" He cheers. Our eyes meet and he rubs his arm. We both laugh. It's nice to remember, and laugh.

#

(March 1965)

The Hullabaloo is a smoky, crowded place. The stage is small and the dance floor is hardly big enough for a dozen people.

The crowd is made up of a little bit of everyone.

There are women in knee length skirts and belted blouses on the arms of men in crisp office wear. There are women with heavy bangs and short floral skirts flirting with men in printed shirts with hair covering their ears like Davids. The two groups mingle together like the shuffled pages of Good Housekeeping and Vogue.

The band is full of soul and guitar. The Rationals lead singer has a rough, entrancing quality to his voice.

The music is too loud. David and I give up on trying to talk and just sit, drink and listen. I can't decide if Carl would like this band or not. I wonder if I could afford a record. I realize all the records in our home are Carl's. I'm about to ask David if they sell records here when he jumps up and points to a girl in a short printed dress by the bar. He gives a signal I can only take to mean that he is going to go try to hit on her.

I feel old as I think about how it must be impossible to try to start a conversation with someone here because the music is so loud. The band plays a cover of a song I've heard before but something about the sway of their version takes me deep into the sound and I close my eyes.

"You can't fall asleep sis, it's not even 11!" David gives me a nudge and slides a pink drink in a martini glass in front of me. "I wasn't sure what you liked to drink so that girl I was talking to said you might like this."

I look at it with some trepidation. The bourbon and the beer I've already finished have me feeling warm and flushed. I look around the room and see quite a few women holding glasses similar to mine.

I pick it up and take a sip. The glass is awkward and the vodka is strong, but the sweetness that follows keeps me from coughing.

"What is it?" I ask loudly.

"A harpoon. Is it alright?" He glances back toward the girl who recommended it.

I nod, he holds his glass up in cheers before wandering back to the bar.

The band takes a break and the sound of laughter and conversation become the rhythm of the room.

I settle back in my seat and close my eyes again, someone taps me on the shoulder, "Are you following me?"

I know who it is without opening my eyes.

I turn, and my face must give something away because Paul says, "I'm kidding, I don't really think you're following me."

His smile is slow and charming as always. "But maybe I'm following you?"

I try to return his smile but it's awkward. He looks relaxed swirling a short glass that probably held whiskey before but now holds mostly melted ice.

"David wanted to come here, he likes this band." I manage to spit out, relieved to say something normal.

I hate how frazzled I am. I take a long drink from the shallow martini glass. My lips and throat warm with it's alcohol sweetness.

"Yeah, my buddies are over the moon for these guys." Our eyes meet and there's a long pause. "It's my bachelor party."

It sounds like a confession.

"Yeah, I heard. David told me... Congratulations." We avoid each other's eyes. He swirls the ice in his glass a few more times then sets it on the table.

"Her name is Mary. Her family is from Ann Arbor, they are some of my Dad's old friends..." He drifts off.

"That's great, Paul. I'm happy for you." I look at the buttons on his striped shirt.

The band starts up again, a soulful guitar pulls people toward the dance floor with a slow ballad.

"Dance with me." It's not a question or a demand. I gulp the rest of my drink and leave the glass on the table.

We move to the edge of the dance floor where the light from the stage doesn't reach us. He holds one of my hands in his and pulls me close with the other. His body is firm and sturdy.

The scent of him is the same from high school and of

the night we spent together. The thought sends blood racing through my body. I look up at him, the music drowns any chance of cutting the tension with words. I tuck my head into his chest and we rock to the music, a soulful cover of the song...

Temptation 'Bout to Get Me.

#

18

My face is buried into the soft, vanilla scented chest of a heavy set woman wearing bright red scrubs as she roughly pulls me to stand from the toilet while yelling "use your legs, use your legs!" into my ear. Someone pulls up my pants while she tries to steady me.

"Okay, let's turn Doris. Move your foot! Move your foot!" She huffs and I feel my leg move outward, my body turns slightly before I'm lowered into a chair.

"Whoo! You about tuckered me out!" The woman says with a smile. Another woman in yellow appears from behind me and unbuckles the plastic belt that's almost up under my armpits.

"Sorry about the gait belt, I guess it needed to be tighter." The woman in yellow says as she rolls up the belt and hangs it on the wall.

"Yeah, I thought I was going over with her when it slipped up like that." The vanilla scented woman replies, and heartily pats my shoulder. "But we stayed steady, huh girl?"

They wheel me out to a small familiar room with a recliner and bed. I strain to see the faces in the photos hung on the wall.

There's a knock at the door, it opens before anyone responds.

"Oh, look, you have visitors! Your daughter is here!" the woman in red exclaims and points to the woman who just entered. They both pause and stare at me expectantly.

Suzy is my daughter, I think to myself.

I smile at them, which is apparently what they hoped for because they stop staring and begin to talk.

"She's just been toileted so this is good timing for you, she should be good for a while."

"Um, thanks." The red haired woman replies. "Her brother is here to visit too, he has brought something we think might help her, he's done a lot of research…"

Another person enters the room behind her, it's an old man with stringy grey hair pulled into a ponytail.

"That sounds great, just make sure you put her name on it and let them know at the front desk. Okay?" The Red Scrub woman announces. "You should probably talk to Joyce in Activities too. She's really into stuff like that."

"Okay, we will after we see how this goes." Suzy comes over and kneels next to me and gives me a kiss on the cheek. "Hi mom."

I love the kiss so I point to my other cheek and she gives me a peck there too.

"We're down the hall if you need anything," the woman in red waves as the woman in yellow follows her into the hallway.

My eyes settle on the man in the doorway again. He takes a few steps in and shuts the door.

"Hey, Sis." He gives an awkward wave.

"David brought you an MP3 player Mom. It has music you like on it, and he brought you some headphones. It's supposed to help your memory."

Suzy pushes me towards the bed, I look up at the man.

He pulls a little white rectangle out of his pocket and headphones from a bag. He starts talking but I'm distracted by his face and the sound of his voice. He makes me smile. He points to some small markings on the rectangle. I reach out and run my finger over the front. It's hard and smooth like glass.

"It's your own personal music player. I got together a playlist to get you goin' but we can make changes if you want. Wanna try it?"

He smiles and shakes the headphones at me. I smile back. He gingerly puts the large black headphones over my ears. He takes the wire and plugs it into the white rectangle and presses a circle on the front. A screen lights up and music plays, it drowns out all the other sounds. My brain settles in one spot.

I know the rhythm. I know the song. I close my eyes. I feel my body moving…

Temptation 'Bout to Get Me…

#

(March 1965)

Temptation 'Bout to Get Me…

The song is ending but I don't want to stop swaying.

"Can we talk?" Paul breaks the spell.

I lean slightly away. "We are talking."

"No, somewhere else." He whispers with his lips close to my ear. "Where I can hear you."

A shiver runs down my spine, the band loudly adjusts some equipment before their next song.

"Paul, aren't your friends going to be looking for you?" I look around for the guys I saw him with back in Ypsi.

"Maybe, in a bit. They ran into some girls so they're all occupied. They won't miss me now." He touches my forearm, the heat from his touch lingers.

What am I doing?

"Okay." I peek around for David, he's nowhere to be seen.

Paul leads me around the bar to a smaller room with a few ragged settees upholstered in dark green fabric. There are various ashtrays in art deco style stands scattered amongst the seats.

Another couple is necking on a settee in the back of the room but otherwise we're alone. The band starts up a rock song, full of guitar, which drowns out the voices from the other room.

The walk has cooled some of the heat from the dance floor and I'm able to consider what could happen in here. My eyes dart around the room, and my mind tries to race but the buzz from the drinks slow it down.

Paul starts to sit but I remain standing so he awkwardly gets back to his feet. He reaches towards me and brushes a lock of red hair from my shoulder.

I cross my arms and step back stubbornly, "So what's going on Paul?" I sound more annoyed than I mean to.

If my tone puts him off, he doesn't show it.

His look is intense, he steps towards me and takes my

hand. I want to hear what he has to say even though I already know where this is going.

"Look, I'm just going to come right out with it because it has to be some kind of fate that we're both here tonight. And if I don't ask, just one more time, then I won't be able to marry her with my whole heart."

"Doris, you are the girl, the woman, I think of. You are the image I hold when I think of my wife. I can't shake it, you are here." He puts my hand on his chest and again I feel his warmth and solidness through his shirt.

"You're always here."

I don't pull away, I think I feel his heart pounding, or maybe it's my own pulse. I wait because I know there is more.

Selfishly, I want to hear more.

"I will wait for you, if you want me too. I will wait and take you on any terms, divorced...or not. Just say you love me. Just say there is a place for me here," he touches my chest with one finger then runs it up my neck to cradle my head. He guides me in for a kiss.

He kisses with fervor. His lips are hot and wet, his tongue presses earnestly into my mouth. His hand trembles as it slides to my waist to pull me closer.

But instead of the passion I thought I would feel when our lips met, I feel only guilt and hard reality. I don't want to do this.

I pull back and push him away. His eyes fight the hurt, searching my face for some trace that I am not rejecting him again. I don't look away.

"Paul, I do think about you. You are where my fantasies turn when I think I can't handle my life. I imagine how you would cherish me and love me and protect me. I think about how you would be a Dad who would never leave and who would always be dependable..."

"Doris, you know I would. I can take care of you, you wouldn't have to work..." he steps towards me again, I hold up a hand to stop him.

"But that's all just fantasy. It's not even what I really want. *I* am not what you really want. You want to be a hero and I want to save myself. We would never be happy in *real* life."

"We could be happy Doris. Just let me show you, I could take care of you."

"You don't understand. I can take care of myself and I want to. What we think we could be, it's not real. I'm sorry. I know I shouldn't lead you on, I should have left as soon as you walked in. But I'm drawn to you because you make me feel special... and knowing you are out there in the world, wanting me...."

Am I really going to say this out loud? "It makes me feel good even though I know we are no good for each other. I know that sounds mean and selfish and it is. But it's also the truth. It isn't love. It's fantasy, for both of us."

Paul grabs at my wrist, trying to pull me close, his eyes plead. I stand my ground.

"If you are honest with yourself, you'll see it. Let's leave it like this, both knowing someone out there loves an idea of us. That at least someone out there sees us better than we see our-selves, as better than we really are. If we get too close, if we try this, we will ruin each other, we'll be ugly and real. Please..."

Paul lowers himself to the small green couch. He takes both of my hands and kisses their palms. His green eyes are wide and brim with tears. I kneel down on the floor in front of him.

"I wish things were different Doris. Whether you are real or fantasy, I love you."

"I love you too, Paul. Please, just be happy. Take care of Mary, she's lucky to have you."

He gives me a smile and a shrug. "Don't say too much Doris, or I won't be able to let you go."

He stands, squeezes both my hands in his, then lets go.

#

(Present)

Faces hover above me. Their voices are muffled, sometimes words pop through without context, "decline," "pneumonia," "hospice," "family," "love," "sorry."

The room is familiar but not my own. The faces are familiar but unplaceable. Most of the people stay at the edge of my vision where their features start to blur. A few come close and hold my hand. Occasionally they sit with their face to mine, or lay with me so I can feel their warmth.

"Mom." A clear voice, a clear face, just inches from mine.

Suzy, I think to myself with relief. I consider saying it but the effort is too great. My throat is tight. I try to swallow but nothing happens. My lungs are heavy and wet. Alarm, bordering on panic takes over. I try to take a deep breath, it hurts, it's heavy, I can't breathe.

There's a faint beeping sound in the distance.

"Mom." The voice again. Suzy cradles my cheeks in her warm hands. "It's okay."

She kisses my forehead, and I believe her. It's okay. The panic starts to subside, the beeping stops. Suzy smiles and squeezes my hand. I try to squeeze back but I'm not sure I can.

"I love you, mom." I manage a nod. I feel a sting as I pull my dry lips into as much of a smile as I can manage.

Suzy crawls into the bed next to me and starts to hum.

The words to *Smoke Gets in Your Eyes* drift through my head and I am comforted.

#

(June 1968)

Carl has already made my lunch and the kids breakfast by the time I shuffle to the kitchen.

"Cafe, madame?" Carl uses a horrible french accent as he pours coffee into a red thermos.

"Oh, thank you monsieur." I reply in a worse accent that sounds more southern than french.

Both kids look at us like we're crazy. I give Carl a kiss and Suzy giggles. Scott rolls his eyes and groans.

"I don't think grown ups are supposed to kiss when kids are around." Scott mumbles through his mouthful of Life cereal.

We kiss again and he falls out of his chair making gagging sounds. Suzy continues to giggle at her brothers antics, milk dribbles down her chin onto her shirt.

"Okay, enough of that silliness. You're going to make your sister stain her shirt before her first day of school."

I lean over and kiss her on the forehead. "Are you excited baby?"

"Yes, but I'm not a baby!"

"Of course not sorry, dear." I pat her head between her pigtails.

I take some pork chops from the freezer to thaw for dinner and have to move cups full of brushes and odd looking sculpting tools from the sink to make room for the chops.

I wonder what Carl's working on. He recently sold a wood

carving of praying hands with handcuffs that I thought would certainly get us branded as heathens but he had only displayed at the coffee shop for a week before it sold.

He's averaging about one sale a month and has pieces in a few businesses in Ypsi and Ann Arbor. He has his goatee back and a set of wide sideburns.

There are two more women on my shift at the factory, which makes breaks easier and has given me a friend, Cheryl. She has a son Suzy's age and her husband went missing in Vietnam two years ago. The Army said he's dead but you can tell Cheryl still thinks he might be alive. It makes me thankful I still have Carl, being a single mother seems impossible to me now.

"Mom, did I get a cookie in my lunch?" Suzy tugs on my pants and pulls me from my thoughts.

I kneel down, "Yes honey, two because it's your first day."

She claps her hands then hugs me. "I love you baby. Have a great day, okay?"

"I'm not a baby!"

"You will always be mommy's baby. You and your brother." I give her one last peck on the cheek and kiss the boys before I go.

In the car, my heart feels light, I finally feel like I fit where I'm at.

#

(Present)

Scott's head rests near my hand on the bed.

I try to will my hand to stroke his hair. I compel my mouth to form words, to say everything is okay.

But my body lies dumb to my commands. The only sound is the loud and raspy rattle of my breath. I give a little cough.

He looks up and I try to tell him with my eyes that I love him, that he is still my baby and I want him to be happy. "Please don't cry for me."

He reaches out of my view and brings a damp cloth to my face. He dabs my lips and chin. The coolness brings relief where I didn't know there was discomfort.

He kisses my cheek and leaves without saying goodbye.

People continue to move around in the room at the edge of my vision.

Occasionally, they speak but I lose what they say among the sounds of beeping and my own breath. Sometimes, I feel uncomfortable, there's a deep ache that I can't move to relieve.

Someone turns off the lights and it's dark except for what light comes through the window which someone left unshaded. The window casts everything into contrasts of white and bluish dark.

There is a shuffling near the foot of my bed but I can't see what it is.

A figure in a black comes into view. He kneels next to me so his face is close to mine. His heavy eyebrows and dark lashes make him look boyish, but the grey hairs and deep creases at the corners of his eyes give away his age. He picks up my hand and kisses it.

"Do you know who I am?" He whispers with a deep raspy voice.

"Of course," I smile. "You're my husband."

He chuckles and gives me a wink.

"I've missed you."

"I've missed you too, babe. Are you ready?"

I nod and squeeze his hand. "I'm scared."

"It's okay. It will be okay. I love you."

"I love you too."

I cling tightly to his hand for a moment. It will be okay.

I take a deep breath and look up to the ceiling. It's smoothness turns to waves, then clouds, then swirls. I exhale and let go.

###

Epilogue

Present - Fall 10 years earlier

When I open my eyes, plaster swirls on the ceiling come into focus. Instinctively, I reach my arm out to my left and find the space beside me in the queen sized bed is empty. The floor creaks as I drag my slippered feet across the orange and brown carpet that covers the bedroom floor.

There is a worn path from each side of the bed to the door from years of routine. I check the calendar and see it's Tuesday. On Tuesday I do laundry, have lunch at The Sidetrack Grill and get groceries at Von's market.

I notice I must have fallen asleep in my clothes from yesterday. I check myself in the mirror. Ugh, there's that old lady again. It seems at some point I'd start to expect the saggy faced reflection but it always catches me off guard. I'm not sure when my skin gave in to gravity but from the collection of creams I have lined up along my vanity, I've put up a good fight.

I grab a half full laundry basket and head to the basement. I lift the lid to the washer and find it already has a load in it, maybe Carl ran it? I give it a sniff to see how long they've been in there and decide I better run it again just to be safe.

With the laundry running I slowly creep back upstairs, nursing a sore knee that was replaced years ago. I make some coffee but can't bring myself to eat the dry looking bar I usually call breakfast. Maybe I'll run into town early and get a real breakfast.

As I drive into Depot Town in Ypsilanti, I find an empty parking spot on the crowded street. I'm confused by all the cars and people. Usually this sleepy college town is vacant before 10 a.m. I notice the Sidetrack is open, which adds to the confusion because it's never served breakfast to my knowledge.

My feet rustle the mid- September leaves, tokens from the few trees that have given up their colors early. I love the sound and make a point to walk along the edge of the sidewalk where the dry leaves have gathered. I purposefully plant my foot on a large brown oak leaf with just the right amount of curled edges to make a satisfying crunch before I reach the heavy glass door.

I wander up to the hostess stand and wait.

"Hi Doris, back so soon?" A round faced college aged girl chirps.

"Uh, are you guys serving breakfast now?" I recognize the young lady's face but no name comes to mind. I search her chest for a nametag and find the shiny tag displaying "Klaire." When did the letter C go out of style?

The girl scrunches up her nose and smiles, "No, ma'am.

I'm not getting up that early. Did you want me to see if your usual spot is available for dinner?"

Dinner? What is this kid talking about? I look at my wrist but realize I don't have my watch on. "What time is it, Klaire?" I ask, trying not to sound as confused as I am.

"Hmm, lemmie check." Klaire pulls a phone out of her apron pocket and taps the screen. "4:48 Did you want a table?"

"In the evening?" I ask before I can stop myself. My eyes dart to the windows but their tint makes it hard to tell the quality of the outside light. I blink at the hostess, stepping back from the stand. "Uh, no, no thanks." I leave fighting back a creeping feeling of panic.

Outside the door I look up and find the sun is still high and a few fluffy clouds drift through the grey blue sky. I know I just woke up, did I sleep all day? Perplexed, I drive myself the short distance home.

As I enter the house I can hear the washing machine finishing its rinse cycle downstairs. The microwave clock agrees with the hostess and smugly displays a green 4:57.

"I have had about enough of this." I mutter to myself and open the fridge to grab a wine cooler. I freeze at the sight of the newly stocked refrigerator. A full gallon of milk, stacks of sliced cheese and an unopened rotisserie chicken crowd the shelves. I push aside a bag of salad to grab the wine cooler and slam the fridge.

"Did I already go shopping?" I can't remember shopping today. I try to replay the day in my mind but I only remember getting out of bed a short time ago.

I jump at the booming chime of the large grandfather clock in the living room. One, two, three, four, five. It is five o'clock, and I have lost an entire day.

Present - Winter

The steamy clouds of my breath make visible the exertion I feel from shoveling the heavy snow. The walkway from my home to the driveway is short so I like to clear it myself.

The extra 4 inches from last nights storm is hard and icy, the walk is more slippery now that I have scraped the snow off of the ice that's accumulated underneath. I search the shed for the bucket of rock salt. I don't know why I'm putting in this effort.

I can't imagine anyone visiting today, but sitting inside the stale house until Carl returns sounds more torturous. After my search proves fruitless I decide that a quick run to Von's for salt is in order. I snatch my purse from the hook inside the entry and check the clock 10:30, maybe I will stop and get some lunch at the Chick Inn.

As I pull out I notice the side streets have not yet been plowed. I feel a pang of anxiety but stifle it with the self reassurance that the store is only a few short blocks to the west. Besides, the traffic is light since anyone with common sense has decided to stay put this morning.

The glittering snow is beautiful and has created an almost unrecognizable wonderland. A few birds pepper a power line and I'm charmed by their chatter until a blaring honk from the SUV behind me reminds me that green means go and I continue through the intersection.

After a few turns I realize that my daydreaming has got me turned around and I find I'm heading in the wrong direction from the market. I make another turn to head back the direction I think I came from but soon the road splits into a divided highway. Nothing looks familiar.

This is crazy, I think to myself. I have lived here forever. This is my hometown. WHERE am I?

I pull over and try to calm my nerves.

Okay, I see a large factory to my left. It looks abandoned. FOR LEASE signs line the fence. A faint feeling of familiarity paces at the edge of my memory but won't come out of the shadows in my mind.

Where am I? Where am I? Tears start in the corners of my eyes.

Flashing lights behind my vehicle interrupt my sobbing. I can't decide if I am relieved or not when the officer walks up to my window.

"Ma'am, is there a problem with your vehicle?" He leans forward, scanning my front seat with his eyes.

"No officer." I whisper. I feel stupid. How can I NOT know where I am?

"Well, this isn't a safe place to be and there is no parking on the side of the highway." He looks at my tear streaked face and softens. "Can I help you, are you alright?"

"Yes, I'm fine. I…just…"

I'm not sure if I can even say it. "I seem to be lost, sir."

It doesn't feel better to have it out.

"Alright, well where are you trying to go? I'm sure I can help you along." He gives a slight smile. A large truck flies by and the officer steps closer to my window, a gust of wind takes my breath away.

I'm thinking about his question, where am I trying to go? He waits patiently as I comb my brain for the answer.

"Home," I answer. I know this isn't where I was trying to go, but it's the only place I want to be now.

The officer looks concerned "Can I see your driver's license ma'am."

I fumble through my purse, pulling out my cell phone and wallet, then hand the officer my license. He examines it.

"Well, Doris. Do you still live at 445 South St?"

"Um, yes sir. For the past 15 years." I add, feeling somehow validated that I can at least remember that.

The look of concern grows deeper as he takes in my face, then his eyes rest on the cell phone in my lap.

"Why don't you let me give you a ride home and we can call someone to come and help you with your car. The roads are a little messy from the storm last night and I'm sure your family would feel better knowing you're home safe."

I really don't want the officer to call anyone but I'm too shaken and defeated to argue.

"That would be nice," I offer a weak and insincere smile. "Let me get my purse."

The officer opens the door and holds my arm as we walk to his car. Vehicles speed by throwing spatterings of slush on us as they pass. I wonder if anyone recognizes me. I think I would rather they thought I was being arrested than being rescued because I was lost.

He opens the front passenger door for me and I plop in. He pushes the dashboard computer back so he can see me then uses his radio to tell dispatch he is escorting an elderly resident home.

I groan as a lean back in the seat. Great, now I'm the local crazy old lady, wait until Suzy hears about this. She'll be ready to sign me up for the nearest raisin ranch. Maybe Scott can talk her out of it, or Carl. Ugh, what will he think.

As the officer pulls into my driveway I see the newly shoveled pathway and it all snaps back into place.

"I was going to get salt at Von's! For the path, be careful it's slippery." I almost clap with excitement at remembering.

"Huh, well, you were a long way off from Von's ma'am. You might need someone to drive you or something from now on, especially when the weather is bad."

A light snow starts and tiny flakes drift between us.

"Who can I call for you Doris? I won't feel right about leaving you here until I talk with your family." The officer is eyeing my cell phone and tapping his boots together.

I push open the heavy front door, I guess I never even locked it.

"Come on in, I can call my husband."

I look at the stove which reads 12:45, my stomach growls. "He gets out of work in soon so he can come by and help get the car. My husband is at the university."

I swipe the screen of my phone and find Carl's work number. As the phone rings, the anxiety from earlier bubbles towards the surface. I hand the officer my phone and look out of the large back window. The tiny flakes have multiplied and it looks like another February storm is on it's way.

THE END